ALSO BY BRAD KESSLER

Lick Creek

The Woodcutter's Christmas

BIRDS IN FALL

a novel

BRAD KESSLER

SCRIBNER

New York   London   Toronto   Sydney

SCRIBNER
1230 Avenue of the Americas
New York, NY 10020

Copyright © 2006 by Brad Kessler

Portions of this work were previously published in
the *Kenyon Review* and in *Bomb* magazine in March 2006.

SCRIBNER and design are trademarks of
Macmillan Library Reference USA, Inc., used under license
by Simon & Schuster, the publisher of this work.

For information about special discounts for bulk purchases,
please contact Simon & Schuster Special Sales:
1-800-456-6798 or business@simonandschuster.com

DESIGNED BY KYOKO WATANABE
Text set in Garamond 3

Manufactured in the United States of America

1   3   5   7   9   10   8   6   4   2

Library of Congress Cataloging-in-Publication Data

Kessler, Brad.
Birds in fall : a novel / Brad Kessler.
p. cm.
1. Aircraft accidents—Fiction. 2. Loss (Psychology)—Fiction.
3. Healing—Fiction. 4. Psychological fiction. 5. Domestic fiction. I. Title.

PS3561.E66955B57 2006
813'.54—dc22
2005054120

ISBN-13: 978-0-7432-8738-8
ISBN-10: 0-7432-8738-X

For Stanley . . . For Mokhtar

BIRDS
IN
FALL

Now I am ready to tell how bodies are changed
Into different bodies.

OVID, *Metamorphoses*

I

ONE

It's true: a few of us slept through the entire ordeal, but others sensed something wrong right away. We grew restless in our seats and felt what exactly? An uneasiness, a movement in the air, a certain quiet that hadn't been there before? Several men craned their necks about the cabin. We caught each other's eyes, exchanged searching looks, and just as quickly—embarrassed—glanced away. We were eighty minutes into the flight. Orion on our left, the bear to the right. The motors droned. The cabin lights dimmed. The whoosh of the engines was the sound of erasure: *Shhhhh,* they whispered, and we obeyed.

The woman beside me clicked on her overhead light and adjusted a pair of reading glasses. She laid a folder of sheet music on her tray. Thin, black-haired, she smelled vaguely of breath mints. Her blue cello case lay strapped to the seat between us. She was giving a concert in Amsterdam and had booked an extra ticket for her instrument. I'd joked about her cello on the tarmac: Did she order special meals for it on flights? Did it need a headset, a pillow? She was retying hair behind her head and cast me a barely tolerant smile.

When the drink cart passed, she ordered a Bloody Mary— I, a scotch. Our pygmy bottles arrived with roasted nuts. I reached across the cello case and touched her plastic cup.

To your cello, I tried again. Does it have a name?

She nodded tepidly over the rims of her glasses.

Actually, she said, it does.

I couldn't place her accent. Something Slavic. Romanian perhaps. She wore a lot of eye shadow. She returned to her music. I could just make out the title of the piece: Richard Strauss's *Metamorphoses: A Study for Twenty-three Solo Strings.*

Over the Gulf of Maine, the moon glittered below us. I wanted to point out to the cellist as I would to my wife, Ana, that the moon hung actually *beneath* us. I wanted to tell her we were near the tropopause, the turning point between the stratosphere and the troposphere, where the air is calm and good for flying; *tropo* from "turning," *pauso* from "stop" (I prided myself on my college Latin). And surely she'd know these musical terms. But the woman was counting bars now. Across the aisle, a man in a wine-colored sweater lay snoring, his mouth opened wide.

Somewhere over the Bay of Fundy the cabin lights began to flicker. The video monitors went dead (they'd been showing a map of the Atlantic, with our speed, altitude, and outside temperature). The cellist looked up for a moment, her lips still moving with the sheet music. Then the cabin fell entirely dark, and a strange silvery light poured into the plane through each oval portal and lathed the aisles in a luminous, oddly peaceful glow. One by one, people tried to press their dome lights on, not yet in alarm but bewildered, to be up so far in the atmosphere, bathed in that frozen blue moonlight. A flight attendant marched up the aisle and told us to keep our seat belts on. The clouds lay effulgent below, edged in gold; another attendant shouted that there was nothing to be alarmed by. The lights blinked, faltered, turned on again. A sigh rose from the seats, and the cellist glanced at me with nervous relief.

The captain came over the intercom then. He apologized and mentioned we were going to make a "short stop" in Halifax "before we get on our way." He was trying to sound unfazed, but in his Dutch accent—we were flying Netherland Air—his comments sounded clipped and startling. He got back on the intercom and added that we might want to buckle our belts for the rest of the ride and—incidentally—not to get out of our seats.

The cellist turned to me.

What do you think it is? she asked.

I don't know, I shrugged.

Her glasses had slid halfway down the bridge of her nose. She squared her sheet music on the tray table. The man in the wine sweater had awakened and was demanding answers. People flipped open their cell phones—to no avail. Outside, the tip of the wing looked laminated in moonlight, the Milky Way a skein above. We had started sinking fast, that much was clear, the nose of the plane dipping downward; and there was a curious chemical smell, not exactly burning, more like a dashboard left to bake in the sun.

The man in the wine sweater bolted from his seat and ran toward the bathrooms at the rear galley of the plane. Beside his empty seat a young Chinese woman in leather pants lay sleeping, earphones on her head, seat belt cinched across her hips. She wore an eyemask across her face.

Someone ought to wake her, the cellist said.

She's better off sleeping, I replied. Besides, it's probably nothing.

Probably, she whispered.

Tell me, I asked, about your instrument.

She looked at me with disbelief.

My cello?

Yes, I urged. I wanted to distract her; I wanted to distract myself. Then, as if she understood the reason for the query, she swallowed and began talking about her cello, how it was built by one of the great Italian cello makers, a man named Guadagnini, and how he traveled between Cremona and Turin, and how his varnishes were famous, though they varied with each place he worked. She talked of the thinness of the plates, the purfling, the ivory pegs, the amber finish he was known for. I could barely hear her voice; she kept toying with one of her earrings. I asked if it was old and she said, yes, it was built a few years before the execution of Marie Antoinette.

She snapped off her glasses and drained the meltings of her Bloody Mary and placed the cup back in its bezel. Her hands were trembling slightly. The Chinese girl hadn't moved; we could hear the tinny sound of hip-hop through her earphones.

For several minutes neither of us said a word. Clouds shredded past the windows. The cabin rattled unnervingly. The entire plane was silent now, save the shaking and the whisper of air in the vents. The name Moncton appeared on the video map. We were being passed from one beacon to the next, a package exchanged between partners, Boston Control to Moncton Control. The cabin grew noticeably hot. The moon was now the color of tea.

I told the cellist I had a particular interest in orientation and flight. In birds, actually. That I was an ornithologist, my wife too; I told her about the study skins and museum collections. She nodded, clenching and unclenching a cocktail napkin in her fist. I rabbited on to fill the empty space, so my voice might be a rope that both of us could cling to; and I told her about polarization filters and magnetic fields, the tiny pebbles, no larger than poppy seeds, found between the skull bones of migratory birds. Magnetite, I said. Black ore, which helps them home, to the same nest or tree across an entire hemisphere. I kept the patter going, reeling and threading out more rope, whatever came to mind, cladistics, the systematics laboratory, how we needed new bird specimens for their DNA (which you couldn't obtain from the old study skins), and how I collected birds (killed them actually), and that I was going to Amsterdam to deliver a lecture and then visit the Leiden Museum to inspect their collection of Asian Kingfishers. I told her about Ana as well, her work with Savannah Sparrows and migration—but the cabin was growing hotter by the minute, my collar sponged now in sweat, the little hairs on my arms damp. The plane shuddered and pitched and my heart leapt and I could hear the cellist's breath catch beside me. "Gravity" comes from the Latin *gravitas,* I explained. Heavy, grave, a lowness of pitch. The impulse of everything toward the earth. Newton's universal law, Kepler's "virtue." Someone vomited in their seat; we heard the vile gurgle, then smelled the sickening odor. The cellist yanked the paper bag from her seat pocket.

Shut up! she hissed.

Was I still talking? I hardly knew. She fished inside her pocketbook and fumbled a tube of lipstick and a hand mirror, and held the trembling glass in front of her face. Her forehead gleamed. She skull-tightened her lips but kept missing, dabbing dots of pigment on her cheeks.

Fuck! she screamed and clicked the compact and tossed it in her purse.

Then she pushed up the cotton sleeve of her black blouse. Her arm was slender and pale. With the lipstick, she composed an *E* just below her elbow. I watched as she wrote each letter on the inside white of her arm: *E,* then *V,* then *D,* then *O.*

When she finished it spelled "Evdokiya."

She handed the opened tube across the cello.

What do I do with this? I asked.

You write your name.

You're being dramatic.

Am I? she asked.

The name of the lipstick was Japanese Maple. Against her pale skin, the letters looked lurid and blotchy.

The Japanese maple on our roof was slightly more purple than the lipstick. Its leaves in fall the color "of bruises" Ana once said. She would have looked good wearing that pigment. I held the glistening tube in my hand, not knowing what to write or where. I wanted to write Ana's name, or both our names, as though we were a piece of luggage that, lost, would find its way back to our loft. So I put our address down, taking care with each number, each letter: 150 First Avenue; and then I showed my arm to the cellist, and she said: Your *name.* Yet I couldn't bring myself to write it down.

The smoke seeped in slowly and curled to the ceiling. The smell of burning plastic was distinct now. The video monitors were still working and showed we were twenty miles from Halifax. A man in a silk prayer shawl stood bobbing up and down in the aisle, the white cloth a cowl over his head. The girl with the earphones still lay fast asleep; no one apparently had woken her. Now and again a pilot or a flight attendant raced up the aisle, urging us to keep calm. We all had our life vests on by then—some inflated theirs against instructions, and you could hear the alarming *pffffff* of them filling with air. The cellist found my hand across the cello case and burrowed her fingers into mine, as if to hide them there. Others were grabbing hands across the aisles. I kept jerking open my jaw to pop the unbearable pressure in my ears; the cellist was doing the same. I imagine, in the end, we all looked like fish.

An eerie whistling filled the fuselage like someone blowing into a soda bottle. The cellist named the notes as we were going down. The pilot was uttering the word "pan, pan, pan." We could hear it over the intercom. It sounded as if he were shouting for bread.

We dropped between layers of atmosphere. Clouds tore past the wing. The whistling lowered to a gentle warble, the fuselage a flute with one hole left open, an odd arpeggio in the rear of the plane. Someone shouted *land!* and I pressed my forehead to Plexiglas and saw, between scraps of cloud, lights below, pink clusters like brush fire, four or five of them, the brief flames of villages and towns checkerboarded, scalloped along the coast, yet distant; and some began to cheer, thinking, We will make it; we are so close to land, Halifax couldn't be far. We were coming over the spine of the world, out of the night, into the welcoming sodium lights of Canada. We hit clouds again and the plane shuddered; the ocean hurled to the left, and the plane rammed hard to the right.

Oxygen masks sprang from the ceiling panel and swung in front of our faces. I caught mine and helped the cellist with hers. The plastic was the color of buttercups.

She took the belt off her cello and unfastened the buckles.

Help me! she screamed through her mask. She was in a sudden rush, fumbling, standing, a flight attendant shouting for her to sit. I helped her prop open the shiny plastic case and saw inside the instrument—amber-toned, varnish gleaming, the grain a fine and lustrous brown. In its capsule of red velvet it looked like a nesting doll. She slipped a finger in through the F-hole and touched the sound post and closed her eyes. The instrument was humming a sympathetic vibration.

It's the D, she whispered.

It'll be safer with the case closed, I said.

She leaned over and kissed the cello's neck and let the cover drop.

The cabin rattled. The bulkheads shook. The overhead bins popped open. Bags, briefcases, satchels rained down. The cellist clenched her eyes. I felt her fingers tightened on mine— but it was Ana I felt beside me.

We broke cloud cover and dropped into a pool of dark. The bones around my cheeks pressed into my skull. I saw the sheet music flattened like a stamp on the ceiling. The metamorphoses. I couldn't tell which way was up and which was down and out the window a green light stood on the top of the world, a lighthouse spun above us, a brief flame somewhere in the night.

Did I feel it then, the beginning of this pilgrimage, from air to thinner air, from body to body, before the impact? Was it then or after or in between, before the seat belts locked our pelvises in place and unleashed the rest of us. The ilium. Why is it the same name for Troy? Ana once asked, tracing the upper bone of my hip with her finger. Because it's a basin, I said, and told her the Latin word *ilia*. More like wings, she said and climbed above me and laid the two points of her hips on top of mine. Our bones tapped together, like spoons.

The cabin burst into light, sunbright, dazzling, an orange edging around it. I could see the bones beneath my flesh like pieces of pottery. And then we were entering the sea.

TWO

The sunset over Trachis Bay had been brilliant, and now the ocean lay pewter in the lingering dusk. It was the perfect end to the final Sunday of the season; families lingered on the beaches until the last possible moment, dragging children—red-faced, reluctant—into vans, locking up cottages, stuffing suitcases, shutting hot water heaters for the summer. They crammed into the last ferry and headed back to the mainland and the cities. It was the middle of September. They wouldn't be back until Christmas—or more likely the following spring.

This was the season and the hour Kevin Gearns liked best, after the crowds departed, the guests thinned at the inn, the beaches emptied again, when the island itself seemed to breathe a sigh of relief. In another few weeks, they'd close the inn for the year. Kevin couldn't wait. After months of non-stop guests, of cooking each night for a dozen strangers, arguing over bills and diets and bedding, they'd shutter the cottages and hang the wooden sign on the Peninsular Road "Closed for the Season." The nights would turn chill, the trees grow bare, the roads untraveled. By the time the first frost arrived, they could finally relax. Douglas was even talking about a vacation. Lisbon, perhaps. Lake Averno. It didn't matter much where.

The night was warm; a cotton of fog hung over the sea. Kevin had come outside for dill but lingered on the lawn, inhaling the wild tobacco, the potted jasmine. Ever since they'd bought the inn on Trachis Island, he'd wanted a moon garden, but he'd had neither the time nor the energy until that summer. He'd planted the night blooms as a surprise, furtively, on afternoons when Douglas was away. But Douglas didn't appreciate the subtleties of trumpet lilies or Himalayan musk roses. Why, he asked, would you want flowers blooming when no one can *see* them? If you have to ask, Kevin felt like saying . . . but resisted. He simply replied: For the moths.

That summer was their tenth anniversary on Trachis Island. They'd bought the inn with money from the sale of Kevin's mother's house in Brookline. Kevin had the most tenuous connection to Nova Scotia: a childhood trip there one summer with his grandparents. Yet the memory of brick-red cliffs, blue water, beaches of white, speckled stones had stayed in mind, stored away, a seed lying dormant all those years. When his mother's estate was finally settled, Kevin knew exactly what he'd do with the money—though he'd never spoken it before. Nova Scotia. The words nearly surprised him too. They would move there. They would find a place, on an island preferably. No matter that he and Douglas were Americans. No matter that he hadn't been back since that one childhood trip. Why not the Cape? Douglas asked. Why not Fire Island? Why not—for that matter—the Jersey Shore? Kevin wouldn't hear of it. So fraught were all of those places with memories and ghosts of those he'd cared for with Hickmans and cocktails—not to mention his abandoned dissertation (left in a box bound in rubber bands)—that all he wanted was to leave everything behind. A fresh start. A new place, a *terra nova*. An island.

But how would they live? Douglas protested.

Kevin remembered his face when he told him his idea for an inn. And what exactly, Douglas inquired, one hand on hip, made him capable of running an inn?

Nothing, Kevin shrugged. But he'd cared for so many sick people for the last eight years, how much harder could it be looking after perfectly healthy ones on holiday?

Besides, Kevin added, he liked the ring of the word "innkeeper." It sounded so Chaucerian.

In the end Douglas consented; what else was he to do? He had no real job to speak of, only the occasional work as a personal trainer. Most of the important decisions in the last few years he'd ceded to Kevin, not because Kevin was twelve years his senior—and a bit more experienced—but because Douglas was too lethargic to make up his mind. So when it came to the big move, Douglas went along, more out of laziness than any real conviction that living on an isolated island suited his temperament or lifestyle.

The property came with eleven acres, one hundred feet of ocean frontage, a beach of crushed pink shells. Broken crockery, Kevin called it, sifting sand through his fingers the first afternoon they visited, for the beach sand looked like nothing more than teacups and saucers that had been tumbled ceaselessly by the tide. How appropriate to move there then, Kevin mused, among the pulverized dishes, the shards of scallop shells, for his life up until that point in New York City had seemed the tail end of an imaginary tea party where all the guests were now gone. That June afternoon, looking up at the house on the bluff, Kevin knew this was the place he'd live for the rest of his life. Trachis. An island ringed by emerald. Black glacial boulders. Fifteen miles from the mainland. Twenty from the Scotian Shelf. So what if, two months earlier, he'd never even heard of the place?

That first afternoon, he and Douglas wandered up the path to the main house: a Greek Revival, with Gothic touches added *later*. The Realtor had left them keys. The house was chill, echoey, redolent of mice. They wandered each enormous room, Douglas reluctant, skeptical (though with a slight mercurial look), Kevin trying to keep himself from ecstatics. The carpets smelled of sea damp. There was sand on the floor, a library with warped shelves, old books with gilt edges and pages pocked with mold (they'd have to be spread in the sun). A Persian rug lay rotting on the parquet. A black Baldwin upright, scandalously out of tune. Plaster crumbled everywhere. Paint blistered. Could they possibly restore the place to its grandeur? The lightning rods beaded with cobalt porcelain balls, the widow's walk, the Doric columns? Yes, it was tremendous work. But even Douglas had to admit there was something magical about the spot: the dramatic drop to the ocean, the lime green of the lawn in early June, the Prussian blue of the sea. To wake to that each morning, Kevin thought, he'd feel alive again after all those years in a lightless apartment on Gansevoort Street.

The first few seasons on Trachis were not easy. There were problems with the contractors, the plumbing, the dry rot. They had trouble finding help; the housekeepers kept quitting. The islanders themselves were not particularly welcoming. Neither Douglas nor Kevin was a Maritimer. Worse yet, they were *Lower Americans*—the worst kinds of carpetbaggers. Hadn't Kevin overheard Bunty Phillips, the island constable, once say as much, publicly, at a town meeting?

Yet slowly, incrementally, year by year, they were, if not entirely embraced, at least accepted. When people drove past Trachis Inn now off the Peninsular Road, they caught sight of the yellow-painted main house, the black shutters, the spruces and antique hollyhocks out front. It looked so much better than before, when the place had lain in ruins—they had to concede that much. For the main house was one of the island's few historic buildings, had belonged to Ezra Trachis himself, a sea captain. His wealth, they said, was earned in the opium trade.

Kevin unlatched the gate and entered the garden. An orange moon drifted hazily in the east. He found the patch of dill, the heads lush, lacy, fragrant in the moonlight. He was making a gravlax from a salmon he'd bought that morning straight off Government Dock. Nova Scotia salmon, the freshest possible. He needed several bunches of dill and some juniper berries for the recipe. Down at the cottages, lights twinkled through trees. Oscar barked and loped on the lawn, nose to ground, the sea behind; he'd caught the scent of rabbits.

The inn was nearly empty after the weekend, the main house

unoccupied. In the Quahog Cottage stayed the retirees from
Minnesota: a lumbering man with burst blood vessels on his
cheeks, and his tiny, wire-haired wife. They'd been motor-
cycling around the Maritimes on matching Harleys. In the
Whelk Cottage were the young windsurfers who came to breakfast each morning in wet suits. Kevin had stumbled upon them
on the beach the night before while walking Oscar. They were
naked in the firelight, the girl acrobatically on all fours, her ass
in the air. Kevin came back to the main house holding a hand
to his mouth.

What? Douglas asked.

Whelks on the beach, Kevin said.

Whelking?

Kevin nodded.

Oh my God, you saw it?

Yes, Kevin said. Regrettably.

He couldn't wait for them to leave. The boy had the tiniest
brown beard hanging from his chin like a shred of steel wool
that practically begged to be snipped off. And just that morning, he'd knocked meekly on Kevin's office door and mumbled
something about a clogged toilet. Kevin discovered later a
blue condom flushed down there, despite the quaint signs he'd
calligraphied himself—perhaps too quaint—that warned of
the delicate island plumbing, not to put anything "incommodious" in the "commode." What didn't they understand:
Incommodious? Commode? Thank God, they'd be gone in the
morning, along with their colored condoms.

Kevin placed the last of the dill in the basket. A scarf of clouds
crept off the ocean—vaporous, metallic blue. He left the garden

and walked to the bluff for juniper berries. On a clear night over Trachis, he often saw the aurora borealis this time of year. On any cloudless night, the stars were overwhelming on the island, and if he looked up he could see, among all that acreage of sky, tiny red navigational lights flitting across the atmosphere. Airplanes, hardly noticeable, tacking across the Atlantic on their way toward Europe or Asia. Other times the Canadian Navy flew practice runs directly over the island, the F-16s thundering so low, so loud, the windows of the cottages shook in their frames. That night was too cloudy, and the moon too full, for the aurora borealis. Oscar sniffed the air, tail erect, and growled. Kevin groped for berries among the juniper needles. The offshore fog slipped eerily beneath the moon.

Back inside, the office lights blinded him. Douglas lay sunk in a Mission rocker, immersed in the pages of a *Consumer Reports*. Their chain saw had died earlier that summer and he was shopping for a new one.

It looks like either a Stihl or a Husqvarna, Douglas announced. He didn't look up; he wore a look, so familiar lately to Kevin, of concentrated annoyance.

The displacement values are better with the Stihl, he muttered. But the price with the Husqvarna. He sighed and turned the page.

Kevin set the basket of dill on the counter.

The Husqvarna sounds sexier, Kevin remarked.

Douglas rolled his eyes.

It's not about the name.

What is it, Russian?

Swedish.

And the Stihl?

German.

Can you get the Husqvarna, Kevin asked, for a Stihl?

Douglas peered over the top of the magazine with an exasperated expression. Kevin picked the basket off the counter and started toward the kitchen.

Well, it's all the same to me, he said and waved one hand in the air.

Halfway through the door, he stopped. Oscar was barking madly now outside.

What's wrong with the dog? Douglas asked, but Kevin didn't answer.

They heard the plane then at the same time: louder and more thunderous than usual. The windows trembled. The lights flickered. And then there was a high deafening shriek as if the aircraft was heading straight into the house. The chandelier shook. A puff of plaster ghosted from the ceiling. In seconds, the roar receded.

Fucking navy, Douglas shouted and threw down the magazine. Why do they need to come in so close?

Kevin, who hadn't moved from the door, who was still gripping the basket of dill, his heart thumping, said: That didn't sound like the navy. He hurried back the way he'd come, through the screen door, out into the night, up the hill, and back to the garden for a better view. Oscar shivered beside him, tail between his legs. The fog had nosed onshore. The groan of the aircraft was faint now, somewhere out at sea.

Years afterward, Kevin wished he'd gone somewhere else, to the bluff or the parking lot, or out to the Peninsular Road—anywhere but inside the garden. For whenever he opened the gate in autumn again, whenever he caught the scent of ripe salt hay or dill or the ginny odor of juniper berries, he'd remember what he saw that night, two, three miles offshore: the bottom of a fuselage lit up in a ghastly red glow, enormous, groaning, something not meant to be there, that low, in that place. To have seen it, by himself, alone, a single witness, and then see it no longer—all from inside the garden gate (and hear the terrifying explosion moments later)—seemed almost a personal failure, monumental in scope. The garden, of all places, where he'd always felt protected, enclosed, engirded among his Brussels sprouts and cabbage, his moonflowers; where the world could never enter, where the guests and even Oscar were not allowed.

Lights flashed on in the cottages. Guests ran out to their decks. Douglas appeared in the lighted panel of the office door and shouted for Oscar (*Oscar!* why not for him?). Sheila Quinn, the kitchen help, ran outside as well, wiping hands on a dish towel.

What happened after was a blur. Sirens wailed sometime later on the Peninsular Road. The retiree with the red cheeks paced the bluff holding a shortwave radio, trying to raise a police scan.

Kevin retreated to the kitchen. When he was a child, in times of crisis, his mother had always brewed a pot of tea. When his father died, when the call came, she went calmly to the sink and filled a kettle, placed it on the stove and sat in a kitchen chair. Kevin had inherited the habit, along with her Brown Bettys and her collection of tea cozies (quilted from the shoulder pads of her vintage dresses). He did the same now. He set a large copper kettle on a ring of blue flame and turned to the table in the center of the room.

The salmon lay spread out on parchment paper in a baking dish. He'd left the fillets there only minutes before—though it seemed like hours now. Numb, slightly queasy, he rinsed the dill in the sink, chopped it, squeezed five limes in a glass bowl, threw in salt, brown sugar, peppercorns. He spooned the marinade over the fillets, smothered them with dill, then laid one fillet on top of the other, like a sandwich. His hands were trembling the whole time.

Douglas burst through the swing door.

Where the fuck have you been?

Here, Kevin said weakly. Where else?

What the hell are you doing?

Kevin laid parchment paper over the entire salmon.

Finishing the gravlax.

Now? Douglas stared at him incredulously. I'm going to Government Dock. They're calling for help. Do you want to come?

Is everyone all right in the cottages?

The retiree wants to come with me. He keeps asking what he can do.

Kevin shrugged. What could any of them do? If they had a boat, it would be one thing. And even then, who knew?

I'll stay, Kevin said. He was slightly annoyed; he'd completely forgotten the juniper berries. He felt as if he might be sick.

Douglas waited; he was about to say something else.

Go! Kevin shouted and flung a hand in the air.

The swing door paddled shut. Kevin squatted to the floor, closed his eyes, and pinched the bridge of his nose between two fingers. The image of what he'd seen he couldn't erase from his head. Nor the horrendous crunching sound, a sound he'd never heard before but knew precisely what it was.

He sat on his heels, two arms bracing the table, and exhaled; then he pulled himself up, ripped a long sheet of plastic wrap from the roll, and covered the salmon. The fillets would stew for three days in the gentle acid of the lime juice, the flesh slowly acquiring a lighter, pickled tone. The Swedish used to bury theirs underground and dig them from the snow when winter came. Kevin carried his gravlax to the walk-in and maneuvered it onto a back shelf.

All night, the horn on Caginish Hill wailed, the same horn that moaned for fires, hurricanes, and once for ships lost at sea. Lights burned up and down the beaches, in cottages and fishing shacks, in all the old gingerbread homes in Trachis Harbor. In the drawing room at Trachis Inn, the TV blared, the windsurfers huddled together beneath a blanket, but Kevin stayed away. At three o'clock Douglas rang, breathless and agitated, from Government Dock. A search and rescue was under way. They'd probably need food. When are you coming home? Kevin asked but didn't expect an answer. Finally, around four in the morning, Kevin stumbled into a chair in the library and closed his eyes. Some nights he went there when he couldn't sleep. With the windows closed, the dehumidifier humming, it was the only room in the entire house where you could forget momentarily that you lived so close to the sea.

THREE

In the early evenings at the end of summer, migratory birds grow restless. When dusk approaches, they fly off their roosts, circle overhead, call from the dark. The behavior, known as *zugunruhe*, or "migratory restlessness," has long been observed by bird biologists. Anxious, expectant, the migrants begin small reconnaissance flights at twilight as early as August. Their disquiet builds for weeks, until finally an evening arrives in September when the skies clear and the wind bears down from the north. When the sun drops precisely six degrees below the horizon, thousands of birds pour into the sky, triggered by a signal not yet completely understood. The birds stream into the twilight and rise five thousand, ten thousand, twenty thousand feet above the earth. They travel by night because the moon is much more forgiving to fly beneath than the hot sun, and they expend less energy, and fewer predators await them in the dark. They migrate through midnight and sometimes until early the next morning. Even the first-year fledglings, who've never made the journey before, know exactly when to depart in fall, and which direction to go.

Miles from Trachis Island, in the Ornithology Lab at New York University, Ana Gathreaux slept at her desk. Dawn was approaching. Already her caged Savannah Sparrows were starting to waken. Though there were no visual cues in the tiny room on the tenth floor—the windows had all been blackened—the birds knew the precise time. They sang in short broken phrases, little flutings. A chirp. A clicking sound. Ana lifted her head and rubbed her face with the flat of her palm; she'd been dreaming of a small black ship.

This was Ana Gathreaux's first overnight of the year. Since her husband was away at an ornithological conference, she had decided to camp out in the lab; there was no point returning to the empty loft at night only to drag herself back to work before dawn. She'd keep bird hours for two weeks, or as long as her sparrows' *zugunruhe*—their restlessness—lasted.

Ana had spent half the night in an absurdly uncomfortable lawn chair, and rising now, she wasn't quite sure she'd last the full two weeks in the lab. Her lower back ached. Her legs were stiff. She stretched her arms above her head in the red-gelled light. Her hair had come loose and she gathered it behind, grabbed a clip from her belt loop—she always kept one there—and clipped it on top of her skull. The previous night had been perfect for migration. The Doppler images on her computer showed ideal conditions over Manhattan and the entire Northeast: there'd been a cold front, a gibbous moon. On the computer she'd even watched the density of birds gathering over Long Island and Jamaica Bay. They appeared as green specks, ghostly, fleeting, a mineral flame. Later, she'd estimate the density of migrants on the screen and compare that with the behavior of her caged sparrows in the lab. Was there any correlation between the two? Caged for six months in a lightless room in the middle of Manhattan—with no sun or moon or stars to steer by—how did her sparrows know it had been a perfect night to migrate to the south?

Ana recorded the time of her birds' waking: 5:04 a.m. Then she approached the cages. They were bathed constantly in the dim glow of a photographic safe light, but the birds seemed to have grown accustomed to the odd illumination. They hopped in their cages, twitched their wings. She opened one of the wire doors, reached in, cupped a sparrow, and brought him fluttering from the cage.

Good morning, she whispered.

He flapped his wings, tried to fly, but she held him fast by his legs between her fingers. He was a male, a first-year fledge. A small, grayish bird with a yellow wash around his eyes. *Passerculus sandwichensis.* A rather unglamorous bird, yet good in the lab. Easy to rear. They grew on you.

Ana had captured him and the other dozen earlier that summer on a grassy inlet on eastern Long Island. She'd gone that day with her federal permits and her black nylon mist nets and four of her students, including Connie. They'd unfurled the nets along the marram grass and guyed fiberglass poles in the sand, and within minutes they'd caught dozens of birds: Spotted Sandpipers, Seaside Sparrows, Willets, a Common Tern. She showed her students how to untangle the birds' legs from the nylon, and how to hold them firmly (yet gently) in hand. She showed them also how to clip the tiny colored plastic collars—the bands—around the birds' legs. Ana herself weighed and measured the sparrows and took a pipette of blood from each she was keeping. She released all the other species (a Piping Plover, a Song Sparrow, a Pine Warbler, even a Laughing Gull) but kept a dozen of the baby Savannahs. She stuffed each of them into its own calico bag with a drawstring and set them carefully inside a milk crate. By afternoon, an unexpected squall blew in from the ocean. To keep her young sparrows warm and dry, she stuffed two calico bags down her sweater and nestled them between her breasts.

Her students looked on in horror.

Come on. She nodded at the rest of bags. Tuck in your shirts, and down they go. All of you.

If they wanted to be bird biologists, she explained, they needed to get closer to their subjects.

Dutifully, skeptically (a few squeamishly), they all sunk bags down their shirts, some beside their bras, others just above their belt lines.

And no cheating, Ana said. *Right* beside your skin, where it's warmest, otherwise it won't work.

For the rest of the afternoon, until the rain passed and they'd rolled up the nets and climbed back into the warm van, the birds stayed nestled beneath her undershirt, thumping against her breastbone. She could still feel the flutter on her chest, like an extra heartbeat. She'd been feeding the sparrows in the lab ever since. Her own mash of grass seeds, grubs, and corn.

The male in her hand tried to fly again, then nibbled at the quick of her thumb.

Shhhh, she whispered and gently blew in his face. Stop that.

She reached into the cage and removed the bottom paper—

typewriter correction paper—and set the bird back inside, and closed the door. The page was flecked with feces; Ana looked at the imprints left on the paper. Tiny forked scratches, sparrow's feet, they indicated the direction the bird had tried to fly the night before. She held the correction paper briefly beneath the light. The orientation was remarkably consistent. The tiny feet made a spray pattern uniformly toward the southwest. She put the page on her desk to input later.

She went to the other cages, removed the typewriter paper from each, and inspected the patterns (all aligned the same, except for one). She weighed each bird, fanned their primary feathers against the gelled light, checked for mites. When she approached each cage, the bird twitched its wings and begged for food the way it would from its parents in the wild. All except one. A male named Rothschild—after Lionel Walter, the bird collector. Naming them was a bad idea, and unscientific besides; but this one her husband had named while visiting the lab one afternoon. The bird stood off by itself, and Russell, poking at the cage, said: What's with little Lord Rothschild? Connie repeated the name; and despite Ana's rule, "Rothschild" stuck. The sparrow huddled now in the back of his cage—a bad sign. He wasn't eating, his left eye was half shut. Ana took him out last and tried to feed him by hand. If he didn't perk up in a day or two, she'd have to destroy him. She'd write a note to Connie. She'd make sure not to use his name.

An hour later, she'd fed all the birds and input the data. She locked the lab and rode the elevator downstairs. The sky tinted rose through the high lobby windows. The night guard sat listening to Haitian radio on a transistor propped on his desk.

Good morning, Armand, Ana said.

27

How is your early birds, mademoiselle?

Very well, thank you.

He yawned and stretched both arms out to the sides, then checked his wrist.

One more hour to go, he said.

A long night? she asked.

They're *all* long.

And the baby? Ana asked.

Armand broke into a weary smile. He removed his security hat from his head, turned it upside down, and showed her the inside. A color snapshot of the baby lay inserted into the plastic lining. She was three weeks old, Armand said. Her name was Alice.

How adorable, Ana remarked.

Armand's gums showed when he grinned. He admired the photograph a moment, then put his hat back on and patted the brim.

I keep her here on top of me, Armand explained.

Well, Ana smirked, *that's* using your head.

The news came on the transistor in Creole, but neither Ana nor Armand listened. Armand once helped Ana upstairs with some cages. He thought he recognized the sparrows from Hispaniola. In Haiti they called them *Moineaux des Herbes*— or *Zwazo Kann* in Creole. Ana was certain he was talking about Grasshopper Sparrows—*Ammodramus savannarum.* Yet she forgave him for confusing the two; they looked awfully similar if you weren't a birder with a life list.

Ana congratulated him again. Armand checked his watch once more.

Fifty-five minutes to go, he announced.

You stay awake on the subway, she said.

I'll try, he offered unconvincingly.

Ana waved to him as she entered the rotating doors.

The morning was bracing outside. She pulled a knit turtleneck and a black beret from her knapsack and slipped them on. The streets lay mostly empty. A man was hosing the pavement on West Fourth Street and Greene. A few early commuters hustled toward Broadway. She liked the early mornings in downtown Manhattan. When she and Russell were first dating, they used to cycle to Central Park in the dawn during migration season to see what the wind had brought in the night before. Sometimes in the evenings, they rode to the top of the Empire State Building and watched the migrants passing in the lights from the observation deck. No one even knew the birds were up there. It was their own small secret, listening to the migrants overhead, so close you could hear their flight calls and identify the species in the dark.

On First Avenue she stopped for a quart of milk at the Korean market. The Mexican was clipping tea roses; they nodded to each other (he too had his radio on, his tuned to sports). Upstairs, the loft was overheated; the sun fell through caged windows, the answering machine blinked; it was probably Russell calling from his hotel in Amsterdam.

She set the milk on the kitchen counter, the knapsack on the floor, and tossed her beret on the table. She opened the roof door to let in some air, and the sound of traffic poured in from First Avenue. There were two hang-ups on the machine. Then a third hang-up. Then Yvonne leaving a message, her voice taut and urgent.

Ana, where are you? Call me when you get this. It's Yvonne.

The fifth message was Yvonne again.

Ana, I *need* you to call . . . Okay?

She waited for the next message, but there was none. Russell hadn't phoned. How strange of him not to. Perhaps he'd tried her in the lab? And why was Yvonne so insistent, so dramatic?

She took the portable out to the rooftop. Horns blared in the street. She was sure Russell would call any moment. He had his paper to deliver at the conference. He'd practiced it just the other night. A paper on the necessity of updating museum collections for DNA and systematics studies. He'd read it to her in the kitchen, standing by the sink, she in a chair. Don't move your leg so, she said. My leg will be behind a lectern, he said. Well, what if it's not? Then it moves, he said, don't worry about my leg. But Ana did worry, not only about his leg but about the entire trip. After Amsterdam he was traveling to Leiden for a few days, then to visit his mother in East Anglia. His lecture was that very evening.

The Williamsburg Bridge shimmered with early traffic. Morning glories shivered on the grate. It was a perfect day for migrants, Ana thought, the wind flailing off the East River, cold and demystifying. A bald man practiced tai chi on a roof three blocks away, one hand knifing the air in front of his face. He was often there in the mornings, and Ana sometimes waved to him across the canyons between buildings, and he'd bow in return. Years ago on Mission Street in San Francisco, she'd taken tai chi classes herself, and she remembered the elegant names: Fair Lady at the Loom, Repulse the Monkey, Grasp the Sparrow's Tail. Yet the practice was a bit too slow for her liking, and she grew impatient after about two months of classes.

After the first ring, Yvonne picked up the phone.

* * *

Years later, Ana wouldn't remember that moment on the roof. Not the tai chi man in his black robe, or Yvonne on the phone, or the precise words she used: "Amsterdam" and "airplane" and "crash," all in the same sentence. The bells of the Ukrainian church on Seventh Street were banging. The traffic stood backed up on the bridge, metal and glass glinting in the sun. The tai chi man was still moving on the roof a few blocks away, and he turned to her at that very moment.

What did he see across the narrow canyon of Ninth Street, over the rooftop not one hundred feet away? A woman clutching her stomach, then dropping to her knees? A woman lying, as if sunbathing? The same woman with the auburn hair he often saw there in the mornings, mug in hand, sometimes with her husband. Sometimes without?

The tai chi man swung his arm in the air. He remembered to breathe, to relax his chest. It was all about throwing every bone and muscle wide open, with no hindrance, letting the *chi* sink lower, especially in this movement, with his elbows wide apart, palms facing each other up and down. Had Ana been watching, had she been aware—or even conscious—she might have recalled the name of the position from the class so many years ago in San Francisco: Wave Hands in Clouds.

FOUR

All night lights flashed on the Peninsular Road, the strobes of fire trucks and ambulances. The search and rescue had begun. The phones started ringing before first light. Neighbors, the Red Cross. The Royal Canadian Mounted Police. Could they put people up at the inn? Of course, Kevin said. If need be, could the searchers pitch tents on the lawn? Yes, he affirmed, Why not?

The news that morning kept changing. First there was talk of survivors, a "soft landing" in the ocean. Then the sun rose and the day began again—a day much like any other in September, with a dazzling sky and a warm wind—and it became painfully clear there'd be few, if any, survivors. Helicopters thwacked overhead. The windsurfers packed and left. The phones never stopped ringing. Now it was the press calling, from Paris, from Amsterdam, from Tokyo and New York City. Everyone wanted a room; there were so few on the island. How had they gotten the number for Trachis Inn? (they weren't in the Michelin or on the Web). The assistant of a famous American newscaster called four times. Could the newsman spend a night at the inn and do a stand-up from the bluff? No, Kevin was adamant. No press: The Red Cross needed the rooms. The assistant pleaded, cajoled, then offered—*sotto voce*—an obscene amount of money, which only stiffened Kevin's resolve. He'd always wanted to use the line but never had the opportunity, and now it gave him so little satisfaction: Sorry, he intoned before hanging up, *there's no room at the inn.*

Around ten o'clock Douglas returned, walleyed, exhausted. He leaned against the kitchen stove holding a mug of coffee. He talked a blue streak about what he'd witnessed the night before at Government Dock. Everyone on Trachis who had a boat had sailed into the fog as soon as they'd gotten the call or heard the crash. Fishermen in skiffs, yachtsmen, lobstermen, all neighbors Douglas knew by name or reputation. Each had gone out into the dark, hopeful, expectant. Douglas had waited on the dock with dozens of others and a score of ambulances with their mini bars flashing, ready to receive the injured. They waited for hours, with generators humming and arc lights angled toward the water. But not one boat returned with a living person. As the night wore on, they heard the crackle of radio reports, the grim news from out in the fog. Yellow flares kept cascading from hovering helicopters, lighting up the sea in a scrim of jaundiced smoke. When the first fishing boat returned, the men onboard could hardly speak. What they'd seen was horrifying: a field of debris miles in radius, bits of foam insulation, airplane seats, plastic cups, luggage. Not one survivor, only body parts, everywhere. Legs. Elbows. Tissue. Douglas helped offload some plastic bags into a refrigerated truck.

Enough! Kevin held up a hand to stop him. He didn't want to hear any more. Hadn't he seen enough the night before?

Douglas took a long gulp of coffee. He was hungry; he was wired; he needed to get some rest.

Kevin disappeared into the walk-in, discovered the tray of gravlax in the back, brought it to the table and peeled away the plastic wrap. The parchment paper lay soaked, the peppercorns glistened, the dill still fragrant, though darker now. The salmon had marinated only overnight, but already the flesh had turned a slightly paler pink. He opened the lid of the garbage and slid the entire fish into the trash.

Douglas looked at him with dismay.

What *are* you doing?

I can't serve this.

It's off?

No. Kevin replied. He held the dripping dish over the garbage. He thought of telling Douglas that "gravlax" meant in Swedish "salmon from the grave." He nodded instead toward the window.

It's from out there. Would *you* eat anything that came from that sea?

He shook the last juices from the plate. It didn't matter that he'd bought the fish the day before. For the near future—perhaps forever—anything that came out of that ocean was definitely off limits.

Sometime later that afternoon, a woman from the Red Cross called. They didn't need the rooms anymore for the search and rescue; the army and the RCMP were setting up by the old naval yard on the north end of the island. They wanted to save the rooms at the inn for the family members, she explained. It took Kevin a beat to comprehend:

Family members?

Of the victims, the woman said flatly.

Of course. Kevin swallowed. They'd take all the family members they could; it was the least they could do. The woman couldn't say when they were likely to arrive. Two days, three days, perhaps more. Everything depended upon the search and rescue—and if any of the 242 passengers could indeed be found—and whether their surviving family members actually wanted to make the trip to Trachis. Of course, she said, the airline would fully compensate the inn. Most people probably wouldn't come, she speculated. But the island *was* the nearest landfall to the crash, and some no doubt would want to travel there—"for closure," she added.

Kevin hung up the phone, a little dazed, and staggered outside through the screen door. The day had turned golden; oak leaves crisped in the salted air. The lawn needed mowing. Oscar snoozed beside the office door, flies buzzing about his head. Normally Kevin would spend an afternoon like this in the garden, harvesting tomatoes, turning over beds, weeding. He still had fall lettuces to plant. Escarole, arugula, some Asian greens. There were the potatoes to harvest as well. But standing on the lawn just then, the inn completely empty, the voice of the Red Cross woman still ringing in his ears, he wondered if he'd ever be able to enter the garden again. "For closure," she'd said; but it seemed to Kevin as if nothing would ever close, that it was all just opening, a wound barely begun. Out on the water, a dozen ships moved several miles offshore, a smudge of smoke hovering above. The sea itself had a distinct acrid odor. Douglas had told him earlier what it was: JP-4 jet fuel.

* * *

The rest of the day, Kevin busied himself about the house. Douglas slept. The sound of helicopters came and went above the inn. If the families of those who'd been on the plane were coming, he needed to make the place spotless, homey, as comfortable as possible. He needed to start thinking about food. What would they want to eat? What could they possibly put inside themselves after so much was taken out?

For the next few days Kevin preoccupied himself with this question. He prepared food: soups and pies and pasta salads, not only for the anticipated guests but for the rescue workers and volunteers that swarmed the island the very next day. Overnight, Trachis Island had become one of the staging grounds for the search and rescue. The army set up tent camps for ground searchers. Press vans crammed the roadsides; emergency vehicles crowded Government Dock. Each morning, Douglas drove a vanload of Kevin's cooking there to feed the volunteers. He remained for the rest of the day, helping load boxes into waiting trucks. Douglas had always toyed with the idea of joining Trachis's small volunteer fire department but felt—not without reason—that he wouldn't quite fit in. Yet those first few days at Government Dock, working alongside Trachis's men, Douglas felt something he didn't recognize and hadn't even realized was missing from his life: He was needed. He was relied upon. He was useful. The work was not complicated, some heavy lifting and helping to direct traffic occasionally with a lighted baton. But the rescue workers came from all around the province; and because in the chaos of those first few days no one seemed to notice or care who he was, he found himself blending in, more easeful, more at home with the island's famously laconic men than he ever would have thought possible.

Each afternoon he returned home, oddly energized, always with reports for Kevin; he spoke knowingly now about wing flaps and Air Speed Indicators, pressure units, and turn brackets. Kevin found his new lexicon a bit alarming—almost voyeuristic—but said nothing. What was the use of knowing any of those terms? It wouldn't make a damn bit of difference to anyone on the plane.

Kevin meanwhile stayed at the inn the entire time. He avoided the drama at Government Dock and Caginish Point. He swept the cottages, cleaned the main house, prepared for the families—whether or not they were actually coming. Sheila Quinn vacuumed and mopped while Kevin scoured each room, editing out books people had left on the shelves. Anything to do with shipwrecks or deadly fires or hacked-up body parts he removed; and for some inconceivable reason there were so many of them—paperbacks on fatal hurricanes, the *Titanic,* the Halifax Explosion (*three* copies alone of *Jaws*). Why this preoccupation with disaster in casual seaside reading? Kevin wondered. He took the books to the garage and dumped them in a wine crate. Then he distributed other volumes in the rooms, books he thought might offer consolation or comfort: poems of Rilke, Seneca's letters (dubiously), Thich Nhat Hanh's *The Art of Mindful Living.* A preposterous book about heaven someone had left behind (who knew, it might help). At the same time, the neighbors with the summer cottage kept calling from Montreal. Could Kevin go over and check their house? They had two young daughters and didn't want to expose them to the turmoil on the island. Kevin told the husband, as soon as he had a free moment, he'd go.

* * *

On the morning of the fifth day, the Red Cross coordinator called again. The families were arriving that afternoon. There'd be seven of them. Maybe eight. Perhaps more. She couldn't say how long they'd stay—or even if, once on the island, they'd choose to spend the night. But she wanted to make sure all the rooms were ready.

Kevin hung up and walked to the kitchen and tied on his apron. He felt all at once, unexpectedly, anxious—as he had when they first opened the inn. He took vegetables out of the cooler, pots from the rack, and lit the stove. The morning was overcast, blustery. Comfort food, he tried to concentrate, that was what he'd serve that night. A pea soup, a macaroni and cheese casserole. A meat loaf. Lots of cake. He needed to get working.

He baked and cooked for hours. A light rain thrummed outside the window. At noon, he showered and dressed, and Douglas returned from town. Around two he made a final check of the dining room. At three, Oscar began barking on the porch. Kevin fixed his hair in the hallway mirror and shouted for Douglas. They were here. He threw off his apron, smoothed his cardigan. He wanted to look respectable, reassuring, comforting. He couldn't find the umbrella in the hallway stand.

Where's the *fucking* umbrella? he shouted.

Douglas came up behind, with a large striped golf umbrella, and they went out together to the porch. A cream-colored limousine had pulled in to the drive, the windows tinted, headlights on, wipers slapping. A fine drizzle misted the lawn. The dog began running toward the car.

Oscar! Kevin shouted. You stay.

The dog dropped his ears and sat and watched as well. Kevin didn't want to appear too eager, too pushy. Standing on the portico, he felt for a moment like the head servant of a country estate in a Russian novel, waiting to welcome his masters back from a long absence in the city; because didn't death, tragic death, bestow a kind of nobility on the bereaved? Didn't they become, for a few days at least, untouchable, venerable, beyond rebuke?

A girl in a black leather jacket climbed from the back of the limousine. Her hair was cropped short and bleached at the ends. She had a piercing near her eyebrow, and her jacket sprouted metal studs on the left shoulder. A young man, a few years older, in a blue blazer, got out the opposite side of the limousine. He had the same pale moon face and determined jaw as the girl. Out of the passenger's seat leapt a woman in a gray pantsuit. She spoke to the girl, tried to hand her a green umbrella, but the girl shook her off. The woman in the pantsuit turned and, seeing Kevin and Douglas, shot a hand into the air.

Kevin walked down the steps to greet her; Douglas remained behind. Betty McIntyre introduced herself and clasped his hand. She was with the Red Cross, their Disaster Response Unit. Yes, Kevin said, they'd talked on the phone. There were tight lines around her mouth; her lipstick was unevenly applied. She handed Kevin a card with a Red Cross symbol in one corner. The rooms, he said, were all ready.

Mrs. McIntyre glanced nervously back toward the limousine. The girl in the biker jacket had wandered down to the shuffleboard court; the boy was smoking a cigarette on the gravel drive. Mrs. McIntyre leaned toward Kevin.

Their parents, she whispered conspiratorially, then shook her head and stared off at the girl; Kevin did too. She was kicking a clay shuffleboard disk with her boot. Kevin volunteered to take them to their room. Mrs. McIntyre said she'd better do it herself. They were Dutch; they'd flown in just the day before from Amsterdam.

Two minutes later, a town car pulled into the drive, and an Italian couple climbed out. Then another limousine followed with an elderly Chinese man and woman, and a thin translator in a double-breasted suit. The Chinese woman wore a white dress. Her husband held a small tote umbrella over her head. They walked to the edge of the lawn while Mrs. McIntyre oversaw the others.

Kevin watched them all climb into the drizzle, each with the same disoriented expression, with hair that hadn't been combed, clothes that looked unchanged in days, jackets that were crumpled and unironed. All looked slightly bewildered, as if they'd lost their wallets or keys and kept checking pockets, patting shirts. They walked to the edge of the driveway and lifted faces to the sea and sniffed the salt air, as if, at any moment, on the ground or in the grass or out in the fog, they might find what was missing. And watching them in the rain, alone or in pairs, Kevin felt a pang of such sadness that he couldn't control himself; for until that point, the crash had seemed strangely remote, something that had happened only to him that night alone in the garden; and since then, as he skulked around the kitchen and avoided the island itself, it had all grown rather abstract. But now, watching each new family member emerge from the back of a limousine, solemn and haunted, he remembered that night again, the windows lit up in the fuselage, the awful crunching explosion, and he hurried back into the house, to the hallway, where he hid momentarily beside the antique phone booth beneath the stairs, collecting his emotions. He blew his nose into a handkerchief. He smoothed his hair. Then he screwed up the courage to go outside again and greet his guests.

For the rest of the afternoon, more people arrived. With each hourly ferry, two or three cars pulled up to the inn. Mrs. McIntyre supervised. She carried a clipboard with names and nationalities and contact numbers. A few other counselors— "care partners" they called themselves—arrived, as well as a priest and a rabbi, and each of them hovered around the house, inside the inn, or on the driveway, hands in pockets or behind backs, while the lights of limousines burned in the rain.

By late afternoon, the inn was almost filled. A black family from Brooklyn arrived. A Bulgarian man who wouldn't utter a word. A Middle Eastern man with a mustache and glasses and a tweed coat. Each of them had chosen to spend at least one night at the inn. Perhaps more. They would all travel the following morning to Caginish Point; it was too late that afternoon for the journey.

Just before dusk, one last limousine showed up at Trachis Inn. Kevin went outside to greet the newcomer. Mrs. McIntyre had disappeared, and the other care partners and clergy had left for the evening. The day was growing dark, the footlights along the pea gravel paths already lit. The rain had picked up again. Kevin approached the car with the golf umbrella overhead. A woman climbed from the opposite side of the limousine and stood in the twilight. She hardly noticed Kevin, or if she did she gave no indication of it. She wore a black beret, blue jeans, a thick mocha cable-knit sweater. He expected someone else to emerge from the back of the car or the front passenger's seat, but no one did. The woman held a small tan knapsack in one hand. She was staring beyond the bluffs out toward the ocean.

Kevin came around the vehicle, cleared his throat, and introduced himself.

The woman didn't turn right away. And when she finally did, she looked over Kevin's head, into the trees. He asked if she would like to be taken to her room.

The woman shrugged uncertainly. Then she said in a small, cold voice: Okay.

May I get your luggage? he asked.

She lifted her knapsack to indicate that was all.

Well, then. He held out a hand. I believe you're in the Quahog Cottage.

They walked in silence down the lawn. He held the umbrella over her head—rather he tried to, but she kept lagging behind, beyond the circumference of the nylon. The wind shook water from the spruce trees. The air felt cool. The woman kept pausing on the walk and looking out toward the sea, which forced Kevin to slow his pace. A bit of cold blue was still left in the sky out toward Caginish. The lights of the main house burned above. Kevin began to talk but stopped himself. He had the urge to fill the awkward silence with his usual patter, pointing out to new guests the view, the garden, what was blooming that time of year (sedums, nightshades, ligularias), the names of the rocks on the bluff (basalt, galena, quartz), the history of the place (Trachis Island, named after the sea captain). Yet he held his tongue; it wasn't easy. What could he possibly say that wouldn't sound trivial? That he was sorry? That everyone on the island felt personally the loss?

They approached the Quahog; it was one of the nicer cottages, down toward the bluff, with cedar shakes and a view of the sea. He'd put the lights on earlier, which he was happy about now, for the lit-up cottage looked homey, a bit cheery almost, in the gloom. They walked up the porch; he opened the door for the woman, shook the umbrella, left it outside, and followed her in. The room smelled of lavender bath soap; the electric heater was on. Kevin took a quick survey to make sure all was in order. A bouquet of pink roses sat in a milkglass vase on the kitchen table. There were two tissue boxes beside the bed (he'd told Sheila Quinn to stock extra in each room). The bed was perfectly made with a white chenille spread and extra pillows.

The woman walked to the sliding glass doors and parted the sheer curtains with her left hand. Kevin started to explain that the main house was open at all times, and she should feel free to use the drawing room or the library, that a dinner buffet was laid there now, in the dining room, and she could help herself. He told her that breakfast began at seven thirty but tea and coffee were available any time. The woman was staring out the window, fingering the curtains, her back toward him, but he yammered on anyhow. He told her about making phone calls and using the computer in the main house, and he thought to himself the entire time, You idiot, why explain any of this when clearly she couldn't or didn't care less?

He fell silent. He fidgeted with the key, searched helplessly around the room for something to straighten.

Well, he said, if there's anything I can possibly do . . . please don't hesitate to ask.

For the first time, Ana Gathreaux turned and faced him.

No. She shook her head, then peeled off the wet beret. She ran her fingers through damp hair. It was long and reddish and uncolored, a streak of iron in one side. Kevin had thought she was much younger but saw now that he was mistaken, that her face was slightly lined, her eyes puffy and squinting. Perhaps it was simply her grieving, how it aged one so.

There is one thing, the woman said. Could you please—she made an indistinct gesture toward the ceiling—turn off some of these lights.

Oh, of course, Kevin said.

He went around the room switching off lamps while Ana Gathreaux turned back to the sliding glass and pushed the curtains aside again. She hadn't been able to see the ocean before because of the reflection from all the lamps against the glass. Yet as Kevin extinguished each bulb, her reflection disappeared in the sliding door and the dusk outside came into its own. She saw spruce trees now, the cedar deck, Adirondack chairs in the blue dusk; and down a few hundred feet, the ocean itself, lead gray and churning; and with the lights all off, she stood in the half dark with the innkeeper behind, neither of them speaking. Toward the west, between dark clouds, a patch of orange blazed faintly high in the stratosphere.

It looks like it's clearing, Ana muttered to herself.

Excuse me?

Ana turned toward Kevin and looked into his face.

Was it near here? she inquired.

Kevin had the sudden urge to tell her everything about that night: the fog, the lit-up fuselage, the awful, sickening blast. But if he started to tell her, he reasoned, he wouldn't be able to keep it together.

He swallowed and answered: It was near enough.

She nodded and turned back to the glass and pulled the sheers together again.

Thank you, she said.

Can I get you a dry sweater, a coat? Kevin offered.

I'm fine, she said.

I'm sorry, he stammered, that you had to visit under . . . these circumstances.

She stood by the glass doors and gazed at her fingernails. They were bitten terribly, down to the cuticles. Kevin wanted all at once to step toward this woman and hold her, not for her comfort—but for his.

He left the key on the table. He regretted saying anything now. It had probably been a mistake. He wished he could just slip out the door. If she should need something, he said in parting, he'd be up at the main house.

FIVE

Ana Gathreaux didn't watch him go. Neither did she hear the last thing he said. When the door shut, she let out a long, weary exhalation and sat tentatively on the edge of the bed. The ocean seethed outside. She could hear it through the closed windows. Her head ached; her jeans were damp. She shut her eyes and pressed the throbbing side of her head with a forefinger. The last few days had been a total blur: the phone calls back and forth to the airline officials, the counselors, her mother-in-law in England, her brother; the chartered flight from Kennedy. In the Halifax airport, the other family members had stood in circles in the frigid sunlight, arms draped around each other, but Ana had insisted on coming alone. There were white roses in the hotel room in Halifax, baskets of cellophaned fruit. In a ballroom with maroon curtains, the rescue officials cited statistics: the temperature of the waters off Nova Scotia that time of year (sixty-five degrees).

How long an adult male could survive out there (thirty-six hours). How long a female (more body fat, more hours). Ana took notes; it was the only thing she knew how to do, jotting numbers, initials, anagrams on a piece of hotel stationery, as if she were in graduate school again. She wrote: SAR, CTSB, VDR, LKP, without even knowing what half of them meant. There were more, but the one that stuck in mind was LKP. She repeated it over and over to herself like a mantra that first day in Nova Scotia. LKP. Last known position. What was Russell's last known position? What was hers? What was theirs the afternoon before he left?

The first night in Halifax she didn't sleep a wink. She wanted desperately to get to the ocean; she could almost feel its pull. She wanted to be closer to Russell. For it seemed possible then—despite all evidence otherwise—that he might be somehow still alive. They'd called off the search and rescue only that morning. But Russell was a good swimmer; he was fit and clever and had traveled all over Asia collecting bird species. Might not he somehow have survived? In the field Ana had wired her Savannah Sparrows with tiny radio transmitters to chart their movements after breeding. She'd lost individual birds for days on end, the signals disappearing until, one day, she heard the blips on the radio once more. Couldn't that happen as well to her husband, just when she thought he was gone for good?

She'd requested right away to go to the nearest place to the crash. The Red Cross people had made arrangements; other family members were going to Trachis too. But it took another full day before she was finally driven out of Halifax. The limousine driver kept the little window open between them— just in case. Outside, the world slipped by without sound:

green hills, white gas stations. Rain on the blacktop. She woke to sunlight through tinted glass. Liquor bottles, strapped in place with belts. On the ferry, she staggered up to the deck and set her face to the wind. It was afternoon by then. She stood in the back of the boat beside the rail and wept, while Arctic Terns forked overhead and a large woman with a cane appeared out of nowhere, placed a hand on her elbow, and embraced her. When the Trachis Light swung into view—silent, minatory, the faro's lamp rounding in the tenebrous afternoon—she wondered, was this what Russell last saw? A beacon, a green flame, a candle. Was this his Last Known Position?

On Trachis, all the houses had colored ribbons tied to the trees and hand-painted signs—drawn by children, it seemed—of broken hearts with supportive sentiments (she refused to read them after the first five). In the dimming light, they passed marshes, spruce forests, iron red mudflats, and then they arrived at the high-peaked inn on a bluff: yellow-painted, Gothic, with graveled lanes leading to cottages half hidden in the wood.

For days Ana Gathreaux had been surrounded by others, and all she'd wanted was to be alone, closer to Russell, by the water's edge, to have a moment of stillness near him. But now, sitting on the bed in the darkened cottage, with the door closed and the innkeeper gone, she felt utterly—acutely—alone. The day was ending outside, the ocean folding in on itself. Like her life, she thought, like linen, folded up and packed away. It was exactly one hundred and twenty hours now since the crash (she'd been keeping track). This is why she came here, she reflected. To see the ocean, the wreckage; to see, more point-edly, what *wasn't* visible. Tomorrow, they'd go to the tip of the island nearest the place where the plane went down.

She stood and unzippered her knapsack. She'd brought hardly any clothing—just a long print dress. She was still wearing the same sweater, the same Levi's, the same bra she'd worn since leaving New York City. Somehow to change her clothes, to shower (even to eat) seemed a kind of betrayal, an acceptance; and if she could only ignore the exigencies of her own body, she might outwit the deadly hours that kept slipping past. She removed a toilet bag from the pack and emptied it on the chenille. A toothbrush, a comb, the Valium Yvonne had given her, the sleeping pills (Halcion) she'd taken from the loft. Aspirin. A tube of deodorant. She removed Russell's wrinkled T-shirt from her pack. She'd taken it from the laundry bag, unwashed, and had carried the blue pocket T with her on the plane as a pillow and slept with it wrapped around her head at night. Russell once told her that Elizabethan women kept apples tucked in their armpits and gave them afterward to their lovers. The T-shirt was something like that. Her own private apple.

She removed last a ziplock bag from the side pocket of the knapsack. Sometime that first day back in New York City, Yvonne had come onto the rooftop and put a hand on Ana's shoulder and said matter-of-factly (because there *was* no other way to say it): They want some of Russell's hair. Yvonne didn't have to explain. Ana knew immediately why. Russell analyzed DNA all the time in his systematics lab—ironically. He studied the evolution of bird species by examining their genetic sequences. He'd often talked about the transformation of a species over time, how one molecule of guanine or cytosine could create a totally different bird, a slow-motion metamorphosis. He gathered study skins—preserved birds—from around the world, both for the museum collection and for his own study of their nuclear DNA. So Ana knew all too well about the hair.

She opened the ziplock, removed a maple hairbrush, and set it in her lap. That morning in New York, she'd searched the loft in a fit of growing hysteria, collecting every strand of hair she found, from the bed, the mattress, the pillow, the bathroom floor—not sure if any of them was his or hers or someone else's (she'd never noticed before the profligacy of hair in every corner of the loft). Finally, Yvonne forced her to stop; it turned out Russell's own Kent hairbrush was sitting right on top of the toilet.

At the Halifax airport, Ana had handed the brush to one of the Red Cross volunteers and he'd taken it so gently, so reverentially, she almost, inexplicably, laughed. They'd given the brush back to her earlier that day; and now in the cottage on Trachis Island, she brought the soft boar hair bristles to her face. They smelled faintly of Russell's aftershave: Penhaligon's. Blenheim Bouquet; it had probably rubbed off from his toilet bag.

She left the brush on the bed and went to the sliding glass doors again. The rain had stopped outside. The ocean roared. Wind chimes tinkled somewhere in the dusk. For a moment, a bit of clear sky broke overhead, and the room filled with a muted amber light. The ocean turned molten. It seemed to Ana just then, standing before the glass, that she'd been waiting her whole life to be in that room, at that hour, alone, beside the roiling sea.

The room fell flat again. The light disappeared. She felt so empty, so drained; she'd cried so much in the past few days there were not even tears left inside. She slid open the glass door. The air smelled of low tide. She heard the hoarse chatter of a kingfisher overhead; it sounded, as it always did, like a bird who'd lost its voice and was left with only a rattle, an unlovely staccato, harsh and insistent. It called again from a nearby tree, paused, and rattled once more. Had Ana looked above the cedar deck, into the spruce, she might have seen it there. A Belted Kingfisher. *Megaceryle alcyon.* What was the story Russell told her once about the kingfishers? She couldn't recall just then, but her breath quickened anyhow. The hairs on her arms stood on end. She opened the door wider and stepped outside. She was going down to the beach.

SIX

In the main house, Kevin checked the dining room. The buffet he'd put out earlier had gone largely uneaten. The macaroni casserole, the soup, the meat loaf, the mashed potatoes. The Italians had wandered up to the dining room and grazed a bit on a salad. The Chinese couple picked among the fruit bowl. The Dutch brother and sister sat desultorily at a table; the girl toyed with a piece of chocolate cake. But most of the guests had not even bothered coming down to eat. Who could blame them? They probably had no appetite at all. How long would it take, Kevin wondered, after such a shock, for a body to return to itself again and desire food? Diana Olmstead, the large woman with the cane, was the only one who had a normal appetite. She caned her way into the dining room, prayer beads in one hand, and filled a plate with salad and vegetables, and a bowl of pea soup. She sat by herself in the empty room, looking out the large, darkened windows.

Afterward, she bused her plate back into the kitchen, and finding neither Kevin nor Douglas there, she thanked Sheila Quinn. Sheila was doing the dishes, her hands in rubber gloves. Some people called her slow—but it was partly her speech impediment. She turned bright red, and nodded at Diana Olmstead, and quickly went back to her dishes.

Little by little, the guests settled into their rooms in the cottages and in the main house. Kevin made sure everyone had what they needed, blankets and towels and bottles of water, while Mrs. McIntyre helped. The night came slowly. The skies cleared; and now it was late, and Kevin lay awake in the master bedroom on the third floor, unable to sleep. Floors creaked below him. Toilets flushed. Voices maundered through walls. No one, it seemed, could fall asleep at the inn. On the second floor Parviz Mansoor, the man in the tweed coat, sat beside the window fully awake, as did the Dutch girl in the room across the hall. The night had turned balmy. The ocean whispered outside. And whether it was the effect of the moon, which just now rose from out of the ocean, or the smell of the tide, all the guests stirred inside their rooms. For five days, consciously or not, they'd wanted to get to the water. For five days they'd lived with the torment of not knowing, and then finding out, that their daughters or husbands or sons were somewhere lost in that sea. And seeing the orange moon lift from the ocean now, like a spotlight luminating acres of open water, they found themselves disheartened all over again. So vast was the sea. So appallingly cold, so indifferent the metronome of the tide.

Mrs. Liang, who'd flown with her husband from Taipei, wandered the lawn above the bluffs. She wore a white nightgown, a piece of white crepe around her arm, a pair of cotton slippers. She carried a framed portrait of her daughter, Tien.

Mrs. Liang had never left Taipei before, and she found herself halfway around the world, on this strange island, so empty, so devoid of people, with only the sound of waves orchestrating in the night. She climbed the steep cedar steps down to the strand. Where was her daughter? she wondered. Was she out there? In the water? In the air?

Parviz Mansoor, whose young niece had been on the plane, left the front door of the inn and walked up the lawn to the garden. Claartija deJong, the Dutch girl, slipped outside the dining room onto the stone terrace and sat in a chair with her knees tucked under her chin. All of them were drawn into the night like metal filings attracted to a much larger magnet. They passed one another in the dark, each in his or her own orbit but unaware of the others. Mrs. Liang with the portrait of Tien felt the icy water on her toes. Had someone stood near enough, they'd have heard her whispering to herself. Yet even if they'd understood Mandarin, what she said would have made little sense. For ever since the night she and her husband had gotten the call, ever since she'd fainted on the floor of their apartment on the Keelung Road—the two of them clutching each other on the carpet—Mrs. Liang had been inconsolable. She blamed herself. If only she'd flown to New Jersey to see Tien, instead of always insisting her daughter come home to Taipei, Tien would still be alive. For days, Mrs. Liang raved. She pulled her hair. It was all her fault. In the last five days, she'd talked nonstop about Tien coming home, about ghosts and ancestors and crossing water in boats.

The moon climbed higher. Foam pearled at her feet. She held the picture frame before her, as if by raising the image into the air, she might pull her daughter's soul from the night.

Back at the main house, the clock read midnight. Kevin

was a terrible sleeper in the best of times, but now, with the house full, he heard every creak and footfall below. He slipped covers off the bed, careful not to waken Douglas, and crept to the window. Restless clouds crossed the sky. Down by the shuffleboard court, a hulking figure paced one way, then the other. Kevin picked a pair of binoculars off the window seat and brought them to his face. Who was he? One of the new arrivals. By the size of him, it looked to be the silent Bulgarian. Kevin had seen him earlier, wandering the lawn in a large gray overcoat. An escort who'd accompanied him from Sofia had tried to bring him food, but he'd refused. The Bulgarian hadn't said a word, apparently, in days.

Kevin heard Douglas shifting in the bed, and dropped the binoculars to his side.

What are you doing? Douglas asked from the dark.

Nothing.

Don't lie.

Kevin lifted the glasses furtively now.

You're using the binoculars!

I am not.

Jesus, Douglas muttered and fell back on his pillow.

It's the Bulgarian man, Kevin explained. He's pacing on the shuffleboard court.

So?

He keeps going back and forth.

Maybe he wants to play.

Stop!

Kevin focused the ring, but it was too dark to see the Bulgarian's face.

What can we do for him? Kevin asked.

Come to bed and stop staring.

Maybe I can bring him something. A drink perhaps.

Come to bed, Douglas groaned, and stuffed a pillow over his head.

Kevin lowered the binoculars and looked toward the water. The moon laid a trail of shivering gold to the horizon.

What can I serve them tomorrow? he asked aloud. Something to distract them, something to make them—I don't know—not feel so bad?

Christ, Douglas hissed. Here we go again.

He whipped the covers off the bed, leapt out, and lay on the wooden floor. On the rare occasions when Douglas couldn't sleep, his solution was sit-ups. A set of fifty at the very least.

Kevin sat in the window seat and dropped his chin into his palm and watched Douglas in his white boxer shorts on the floor.

There's this lovely scene in *The Odyssey,* Kevin began, where two men—I forget who—are remembering all their friends who died in battle. Helen slips something into the men's drink so they can have a pleasant sleep and forget their troubles.

She slips them a Mickey? Douglas asked.

No, not quite. It's some kind of food or herb called "nepenthe."

You remember this?

I remember this.

Douglas wheezed: How can I forget? The Famous Ph.D.

He was up to twenty sit-ups, the floor creaking with every crunch. After a moment he added: So what else?

Well, Kevin continued. The gods sometimes granted sleep also. It was one of those things they could do, close the eyes of mortals. But the nepenthe would make them forget all their sorrows, for a few hours at least.

Sounds like Ecstasy, Douglas remarked.

Kevin ignored him. That's the challenge, he thought, to serve them a meal, one dinner, something that will intoxicate them, distract them, bring them back to their bodies. He stood now and looked out the window again. The man was still pacing the shuffleboard court, hands in the pockets of his coat. Douglas was up to forty-two sit-ups.

I'm going to bring him something, Kevin announced.

Who?

The Bulgarian.

Douglas got off the floor and went to the window too. His chest was heaving from the sit-ups and he elbowed sweat from his face, then placed two moist hands on Kevin's shoulders.

I'm going to bed, he said. Are you coming?

In a minute, Kevin answered distractedly. He was still staring out the window.

Douglas pinched the muscles on Kevin's shoulders, and Kevin nearly leapt. He was so tense, so hair-trigger (the house so full) and no one—least of all Douglas—had touched him in so long. He pulled away and searched for his slippers in the dark.

I won't be long, Kevin lied, cinching the robe around his waist.

Douglas mumbled something and headed back to bed. Kevin nosed his feet into slippers. The bedsprings twanged as he slipped out the door.

Downstairs, the lights were burning in the hallways. Someone had left the front door open. He went through the drawing room, shutting off lamps, closing windows, and through the dining room and entered the library off the back hall. What could he bring the Bulgarian? Some kind of nightcap, a soothing broth, a calming tea? He switched on a sconce in the library, walked to the cookbooks—he liked to collect them at estate sales—and pulled down volumes. The Fannie Farmer, the Brillat-Savarin, Elizabeth David. He checked the Platina, the Epicurean (he knew of him from his days as a classics student). There was nothing in the indexes under "Nepenthe." He pulled down an old volume of *Food and Cookery for the Sick and Convalescent* and flipped through yellowed pages. Under "Sleeplessness Distress," he found a recipe for "Velvet Cream" and one for "Sleep Aid Concoction."

In the kitchen, the stockpots had been scrubbed, the rubber mats hung over the sides of the sink. He lit the stove, set a copper pot on the burner. The velvet cream would have to wait; for now he heated milk, orzata, shook cinnamon, grated nutmeg, poured a splash of whiskey, then another splash—and one more for good measure: his own prescription. When the mixture was steaming and tiny bubbles gathered at the edge of the pot, he lifted it from the stove and poured the scalding liquid into a ceramic mug.

Outside the night was mild. Clouds raced overhead. He walked through the damp grass in his slippers, but when he reached the shuffleboard court, the Bulgarian was gone. The lawn lay empty. He stood a moment under the moon with the drink in hand. The surf was out; he could tell by the gentling of the waves. He wandered down toward the stone terrace outside the dining room. Someone was sitting alone at one of the tables. Moonlight shined faintly off the studs of a biker's jacket. It was the Dutch girl; she was smoking a ciga-rette in the dark.

Hi, Kevin said. He was suddenly self-conscious. He was still wearing his bathrobe. His leather slippers had gotten completely wet.

The girl nodded to him and exhaled a seam of smoke. Her cheeks looked wet in the moonlight.

Can't sleep? he asked.

She shook her head.

Neither can I.

She smoked and exhaled. Kevin didn't know what to say. He set the mug on the table in front of her.

Here, he offered, It's a little something to help you sleep.

She looked up at him in the dark. Her eyebrow ring shined dully.

This is for me?

If you want it, you don't have to.

She shrugged noncommittally, then dropped the cigarette on the terrace and ground it with a heavy boot. What was the drinking age in Holland, Kevin wondered; and how old could the girl possibly be? Sixteen? Seventeen? It was hard to tell with the dyed hair and the leather jacket.

She cupped the mug in both hands and brought it to her lips and lowered it again.

Is it all right? Kevin asked.

She shrugged without conviction.

What's in it?

Mostly milk.

He didn't mention the whiskey, and she looked at him a moment as if trying to gauge something.

It's okay, she finally uttered and brought the mug to her face again.

They were both silent a moment. The sound of crickets came from the lawn. The Dutch girl hooked a piece of hair behind one ear and nodded toward the lawn.

Look, she said.

A white figure was moving beside the bluffs, ghostly beneath the moon, the ocean sparkling behind. It was Mrs. Liang walking through the grass, clutching the framed photograph of her daughter. She passed a few yards in front of the terrace, talking the entire time in a low, beseeching voice, yet neither Kevin nor Claartija deJong could hear what she was saying. She drifted past them, up to the gravel drive, and then was gone from sight.

Creepy, Claartija observed.

Perhaps I should get her a drink too, Kevin mused aloud.

Claartija didn't answer but sipped quietly from her mug.

Yes, Kevin thought, she could use a drink. We all could use a drink. He wrapped the robe tighter around his waist, excused himself, and went back to the kitchen to make another nightcap.

SEVEN

na Gathreaux woke in the dark, thinking she was back
with her birds in her lab. When she heard the ocean
through the screens, she realized otherwise and tried
to fall asleep again—but couldn't. An hour later the dawn still
hadn't come; yet finally, after six, she stumbled outside to the
deck. The sky was slate, a slash of burnt orange in the east.
Northwest winds. Another excellent night for migration, Ana
thought ruefully. Some dark specks hurried across the water,
birds heading back to land. Often they got wind-drifted twenty,
thirty miles out to sea during a night of migration. In the morning, when the sun rose, they corrected their course and flew
swiftly back to the coast.

Mornings had become the worst for Ana. For six days she'd
woken with a racing heart, remembering what she'd forgotten
in the night: that Russell wasn't beside her in bed, that he was

missing, somewhere out in the water, probably—definitely—not coming back. Each morning a blade sank into her heart and she buried herself beneath blankets, chest pumping, teeth grinding, until she felt as if she'd explode. The only thing was to force herself up, walk around, brew a lot of coffee with a lot of milk and a lot of sugar in it—not the usual English breakfast tea she always drank with Russell.

At eight, she dragged herself to the main house for breakfast. She wasn't hungry. She was too anxious about the trip that morning to the crash site yet thought she should consume *something*. She picked an apple from a bowl, a croissant. She probably wouldn't eat either; at least she'd have something for the gulls. Some of the others—the Italian couple, the Brooklyn family—were sitting in the dining room. She didn't particularly feel like talking to anyone. The Brooklyn family were eating eggs and bacon. They waved her over, but she gestured toward the door, that she had to go. She'd talked to one of the adult sons in Halifax. Their father had been on the flight. He was an entertainment lawyer. He'd worked just three blocks from her lab at NYU.

At nine, two minibuses pulled into the drive. Ana found a seat beside a window halfway toward the rear. She recognized some of the passengers: a Hasidic boy and his mother. The large Bulgarian in the overcoat. Others had come from the mainland for the day. The bus was filling up. Diesel gurgled; the windows were tinted bronze. The man in the tweed coat asked if the place beside her was occupied. No. She picked up her knapsack and stowed it beneath her legs. He thanked her and slipped into the seat.

They pulled onto the Peninsular Road. Spiderwebs glistened in fields. All of the passengers sat with cardboard coffee cups steaming in the laddered light, staring out the windows, lost in their own thoughts. Like Ana, they'd arrived the evening before in the dark and the rain and had seen little of the island. But now, in the daylight, they stared at the ocean sparkling on the right. Milkweed floated across the road. Some late monarch butterflies lifted over meadows. The man in the tweed coat sighed beside Ana.

It's almost offensive, he uttered.

Ana turned from the window.

What is?

How pretty the place is.

He shook his head. He wore a mustache, elegant wire-rimmed glasses; his eyes behind them were greenish. Ana smiled dolefully.

Yes, she nodded, isn't it?

The man took off his glasses and dabbed the corner of his eye with a sleeve. His hair was frosted at the sides, as if he'd stood in front of a Frigidaire too long Who had he lost? Ana wondered but didn't ask. Did the specifics matter? Hadn't they all lost the same? She turned back to the window. A green heron rose across the road. The man was right about the beauty: she hadn't expected that either.

They rode in silence. Music piped over the bus stereo, low and indistinct. Pink and blue houses huddled beside the sea, laundry flapping in front yards, and more ribbons tied around trees and handwritten signs Ana refused to read.

In another twenty minutes, Mrs. McIntyre rose in the front of the bus. They'd spend a few hours at Caginish Point she announced. They were free to wander the site but should keep away from the rocky shore (the surf was quite dangerous, she explained). There'd be a short ceremony at noon under a tent.

The prime minister would be there. She said more, but Ana wasn't listening any longer, and neither were most of the others. They pressed faces to glass, clutched hands, shifted legs in their seats. They were nearing the place; they all could feel it. Outside, the provincial police directed traffic. The road grew thick with emergency vehicles. Army trucks. Police vans. Satellite dishes bloomed from the back of uplink trucks. Cameramen ran into position. A nun and a priest knelt by the side of the road, each holding a wooden cross in the air.

Ana steeled herself. She stuffed her knapsack beneath the seat, put on her beret; she wished she'd brought a pair of sunglasses. Pars Mansoor offered her a blue windbreaker, but she declined. Outside, they couldn't see the ocean yet, but the wind snapped around her, surprisingly cold. People were shouting questions, angling booms overhead.

Keep together! Mrs. McIntyre yelled.

Two walls of people crowded close and linked hands, forming a corridor for them to pass through. Some wore nylon bibs with the Red Cross logo. It was all so confusing. Ana turned to Pars.

Who *are* these people? she asked.

They've volunteered.

For what?

To keep the press away.

The Dutch girl muttered: We're fucking celebrities.

Mrs. McIntyre waved them on. Ana clutched Pars's elbow; she didn't even realize it. They were ushered behind police barricades. An enormous white tent rose on the rocks a hundred feet from the water. Naval officers in bleached uniforms stood in formation, hats over hearts, brass buttons winking in the sun. Someone said: an honor guard.

What would Russell think of all this? Ana wondered. All these people who had come to watch, to help, to gawk. All the signs along the roads, the complete strangers who'd tearfully handed her flowers in Halifax. She'd been touched; she'd been angry; she'd been moved—time and again. But this seemed a ritual hazing, a wedding reception line. What was it about violent mass death that brought everyone out of the woodwork? Hundreds died each hour, each day, in hospitals, on freeways, and no one showed up to witness or weep. Why had all these people come now?

They passed through the gauntlet and out into the relative privacy of the rocks. Under the white tent, tables lay piled high with holly wreaths, bouquets of roses, pieces of paper to write notes on, small teddy bears for children to toss into the sea. On one table stood dozens of bottles of corked seawater for the families to take home. Ana wanted none of it, not the wreaths or the roses or the water; if anything, she'd want to toss herself into the sea.

I'm going down to the rocks, she announced.

Pars said, Good idea, he'd join her.

They wandered away from the others, through the low heath, past large slabs of granite. Tiny pitcher plants shivered in the cracks between the rocks. Some of the boulders were black; others white. Signs in several languages warned to keep off the black ones.

Why just the black rocks? Ana pondered out loud.

She didn't expect an answer. Pars sank his hands into the pockets of his windbreaker.

I wouldn't know, he shrugged. It's like a chess game? One is more slippery than the other?

Ana wanted to feel the water on her face. She picked her

way to where the rocks became smoother and cupped pools of seawater, the green of radiator fluid. Mounties stood stationed every few yards to keep people from the edge of the rocks. The water itself was cordoned off with yellow police tape. The entire Atlantic, Ana thought, was a crime scene.

She squinted into the hard wind. The tape flapped; the ocean glittered like sheet metal. A few miles out to sea, ships moved back and forth below buttery clouds. How ordinary, how insignificant it seemed, the spot itself, out there, two, three miles offshore. Even as late as the day before, Ana had held out the smallest titer of irrational hope, but now, seeing the spot on the ocean, the rescue boats, the helicopters, the rows of naval officers saluting her (as if *she'd* done something heroic), the teddy bears and bouquets of flowers, Ana felt something crack inside her, something she hadn't even known was still there: a last holdout of hope. A tiny twig, a bird bone, toothpick-thin; and it was as if just then, standing on the boulders, she heard it snap.

She ducked under the police tape. Pars called after her. She made a dash for the water. How liberating it would be. How easy. She wanted to get closer, to feel what Russell had felt (perhaps he was feeling it still), the temperature, the taste of salt, the bone chill. Bulbets of green moss clung to the slick rocks, barnacles, and mussel clusters. Already she felt the icy spray. A wave exploded two stories high—malachite, bottle glass green—and rained down on her. One of the Mounties shouted from above, his two hands parentheses around the O of his open mouth. The spray hit her broadside, nearly knocking her over. What would it be like underneath? One leap could take her there, inside the ocean, closer to Russell. A gull shot past, a Great Black-backed. The Mountie was suddenly at her side, gripping her arm.

Ma'am! he shouted. You can't stay here!

He had a stubborn, pleading look. His hat was off, his head shaven, peach-fuzzed like a toddler's. She let him drag her up the rocks. The surf boomed below. She felt giddy; she wanted to scream.

When she returned under the yellow tape, Pars had a half smile on his face. He held out the blue windbreaker.

I think you'll need this now.

She didn't argue; she let him help her put it on and she told the Mountie she'd be good now, she'd stay put. Pars looked at him and said he'd watch her.

Ana's teeth chattered. Her jeans were partially drenched.

You're baptized, Pars observed.

I found out why only the black rocks.

So did I, Pars responded.

They both said at the same time: Because they *are* slippery.

Fifty feet away, Diana Olmstead watched Pars and Ana and the Mountie below. She sat on a boulder, her cane to one side. For such a large woman, she looked remarkably elegant, sitting upright, one leg crossed, the other dangling over the rock. She too had been waiting to be near the site, to be near *them*. For she was convinced her sister was out there over the ocean, along with all the other souls of the dead. She could feel it at that moment, the air slightly electric, as if a current were humming overhead. She'd had this feeling many times before, when her granddaughter had been born and she was in the hospital room, when her own husband died at home in bed: the same door that both life and death passed through.

She sat quietly on the rocks, her eyes half closed, fingers lightly cradling a string of prayer beads. She'd brought the beads back from Dharamsala, each one carved from the bodhi tree, anchored with a tiny hammered silver ball and a small tassel of dyed yak wool. She fingered the string with her right hand as she recited the little she remembered of the *Bardo Todrol Chenmo,* from the Tibetan Book of the Dead—which she'd studied for a year in Dharamsala. It was important particularly at that moment, just as it was when she'd first learned the news, to be calm and focused, to be free from negative thoughts. For this was the delicate time, the narrow time, the intermediate state, when the souls of the dead needed help; and by reciting the words over and over—a kind of Kaddish, a friend once called it—she gave guidance and comfort to the dead, especially those who'd died violently and unexpectedly, those who needed it the most. The chanting helped the dead pass from their present form into their next incarnation.

Diana Olmstead closed her eyes. The sea wind blew in her gray hair. From time to time she looked out at the water, or watched the others below: Pars, Ana. The family from Brooklyn, who stood in a circle now, holding hands and singing. At that moment, with the wind in her face, she felt an enormous sense of peace despite all the death. She could explain this to no one, but ever since her sister died, she'd felt moments of inexplicable joy. It wasn't that her sister, nearing seventy, had had bone cancer and the crash had ended her life only a bit sooner than expected. She grieved for her and all the others, for the last terrifying moments of their lives, and for those they'd left behind. But there was something else that accompanied the tragedy, a certain quickening of life she felt with the proximity of so much death. She'd observed this before: how—ironically—it took death to make one feel momentarily alive, truly present, minute to minute. And there was another thing: the outpouring of love that had surrounded her since she'd arrived in Nova Scotia. *That* was real, undeniable, just as the grief was real too. They were simply opposite sides of the same coin.

On the rocks, she felt it now, a tremor in the air: the souls of the dead hovering over the water. Ana Gathreaux, who was just passing below her, felt something too, a slight quaking, as if the air around her had been sucked into a vacuum. But Ana dismissed it as the cold, the wind (seawater in her middle ear); still, she had to pause. Her legs felt shaky. She leaned against a boulder and closed her eyes. Pars came from behind and asked gently if she was okay. Ana swallowed hard and said— she was fine.

The Dutch girl sat on a nearby outcropping. Ana had met her the day before in Halifax, in the lobby bathroom of the Lord Nelson Hotel (both blowing their noses at the sink). Despite the biker jacket, the black fingernail polish, the patchouli, the girl looked so vulnerable, so alone, that Ana felt instantly protective of her. She was young enough to be Ana's own daughter.

Ana staggered up to where she sat and rested against the same outcrop.

Where's your brother? Ana asked.

Claartija deJong gestured with her chin toward the water. A bit of black eyeliner had leaked down her right cheek. A hand-rolled cigarette sat tucked behind one ear. Pars caught Ana's eye, then pointed toward the cigarette.

Do you have another of those? he asked.

The Dutch girl nodded and turned to Ana.

You too?

Ana hadn't smoked since graduate school, but she shrugged and said: Why not?

The girl pulled a pack of Drum from her leather jacket, pinched tobacco into paper, and expertly rolled a cigarette and ran her tongue along the edge. She offered it to Ana. Then rolled another for Pars and plucked her own from behind her ear. She elbowed herself off the rock, produced a pink lighter and thumbed the roller, but the flame kept quitting in the wind.

Here, Pars said.

He stepped close to the girl, wrapped his fingers around her small palms, and made a perfect cave with his own.

Now try.

She thumbed the lighter, and this time the fire stayed, a flower inside their four hands. A stamen of flame.

Ana bent to the lighter—a bee sucking nectar—and came away with a glowing cigarette; Pars gestured for Claartija to go ahead, and she dipped hers inside, and he lit his last; all three of them with their own fires; and this seemed to Ana a small accomplishment, a campfire, something to ring them-selves around. The smoke from their cigarettes caught the quartering breeze, and they watched it disperse—three scarves of smoke—emptying across the rocks.

Down below, people dotted the boulders now. The Hasidic boy led his mother to the water's edge, took something from his pocket, and tossed it gingerly into the surf. A woman accompanied a small girl in a purple dress to the same spot. The girl clutched one of the teddy bears from the tent. She tried underhanding the bear into the water, but it fell only halfway and landed on one of the slippery rocks. The girl pointed to the stuffed animal and stamped her feet. Clearly she wanted to retrieve it and try again so it could join the other bears already tossed into the sea. It was too hazardous on the rocks, however, and her mother wouldn't let her go, and the girl began to wail.

Pars, who'd been watching the scene, ground his cigarette against a rock, and started toward the boulders.

What are you doing? Ana inquired.

He didn't answer. He was already jogging across the rocks.

Claartija picked a piece of tobacco from her tongue.

Fucking bears, she mumbled.

They watched Pars in his tweed coat; he looked suddenly athletic, leaping from boulder to boulder, backlit, the surf splashing. He was down by the girl and her mother. Ana watched with growing dread. He had to time each leap. The Mountie had run over—the same one who had chastised Ana— and was shouting now at Pars. Pars looked like a high-wire artist, arms held out at either side.

Christ, Ana whispered and wondered what kind of ritual this was, the drowning of plush toys. A gull plunged at the bear. Pars slipped, recovered, reached the toy, and tossed it over his head out to sea.

Ana exhaled; she hadn't even realized she'd been holding her breath. She dropped the cigarette and slumped against the boulder. The Dutch girl shook her head.

Fucking bears, she muttered again.

In another minute Pars returned, panting, beaming, his trousers wet.

That was foolish, Ana remarked, a little too harshly.

Yes, you're quite right.

Ana pulled off the windbreaker and handed it back to Pars.

Your turn, she said.

I'm okay.

Ana clutched her arms around her ribs.

I'm going back to the bus, she announced.

Yes, Pars agreed, teeth chattering. It is a bit chilly.

Claartija pushed her bangs behind her ears and gave them a small nod good-bye.

On the way back to the bus, Mrs. McIntyre stopped them. She was searching for the Chinese lady; her husband apparently had lost her in the crowd.

Ana scanned the rocks. Pars did too. No, they said, they hadn't seen her.

Well, she must be here *somewhere,* Mrs. McIntyre said brightly and squeezed both their arms; then she told them the ceremony under the tent was about to begin. Ana had taken an unfair dislike to the woman at the airport. She couldn't say why. Perhaps it was the tin of Altoids she kept offering Ana. She'd wondered: was her breath *really* that bad?

Back at the minibus, the driver let them in and shut the door. The carriage was warm, the heat blowing in vents. The Bulgarian in the overcoat sat in the backseat where they'd left him, staring out the window at the sea. Beside him slouched the man in mirrored sunglasses who'd escorted him the day before. Ana was about to sit when she marched down the aisle. She didn't know who to ask: the Bulgarian or his escort. She decided to address the Bulgarian himself.

Do you want to come outside for a minute? she asked. I can take you.

The man didn't move. He stared out the window into the near distance. The escort thanked her and said it was okay, that Mr. Raskolov preferred to stay inside the bus. She glanced at the large man in the overcoat again. He had a boxer's nose, tight black curls in a horseshoe shape around an otherwise bald head. There was a cloud of condensation on the glass where his mouth had been. His forehead was lightly glazed with perspiration.

Well, Ana said. If he wants to go, I'd be happy to take him. My husband was—Ana made a vague gesture with her left hand.

The Bulgarian turned from the window and met her eyes for just a second, then looked away.

Thank you, madam, the escort said. Mr. Raskolov I'm sure appreciates it.

Ana shrugged, trudged back up the aisle, and collapsed in her seat.

Some time later, the others wandered back to the bus. The Brooklyn family came aboard, blowing noses. They smelled of the cold. The Italians. The Hasidic boy. The Chinese couple (the woman had been found down by the rocks). The driver shut the door, and Mrs. McIntyre did a head count, mouthing numbers beneath her breath, and soon they started back to the inn.

Pars sat beside Ana again, worrying a small purple stone in his hand. The sky had turned threatening; how quickly the weather changed along the coast. Blue lupines leaned along the roadsides, most already gone to seed. The Trachis Light swung into view.

Is it your husband? Pars suddenly asked.

Who?

He pointed to the gold band on her finger.

Yes, she nodded and stared out the window again.

He probably saw this, she said, the lighthouse. One of the last things, a green light at the edge of the world.

Pars reached into his tweed coat, pulled a photograph from his inside pocket, and laid it on Ana's knee.

My niece, he nodded.

She picked up the photo. It was an old Kodak print, with a white scalloped border, of a girl's head slightly out of focus. The girl had raven hair and was laughing, and the ocean in the background was opalescent green.

She looks like you, Ana observed.

People say that.

He put a finger on the photograph.

It's the Persian Gulf, he explained, there in the background.

I see, Ana said. She didn't want to say: The sea is swallowing her up, even then.

Ana took her knapsack from beneath the seat, unzippered the front section, and pulled out her address book. She removed from the fold the photograph of Russell she'd been carrying for days. It was taken on a mountain in Maine on a research trip. He held a Bicknell's Thrush in hand, and was making a goofy face, mimicking the expression of the frightened bird. She handed the photograph to Pars.

What kind of bird is it? he asked.

A thrush.

It's a beautiful word, isn't it? he said. Thrush. In Farsi it's *basmarak.*

Farsi?

Persian, he explained.

Oh. Ana nodded. So *that* was his accent: Iranian.

Ana introduced herself. Pars told her his name, and they handed back each other's photographs.

May I ask you, Pars inquired after a pause, have they found him yet?

My husband?

Yes.

She bit her bottom lip and shook her head.

Lailah too, he said, she hasn't been found either.

They both fell silent. Pars stuffed his photograph back in his coat pocket. Outside the day had gone gray, blue asters along the road, white bouquets of angelica. Ana mouthed the word "angelica" to herself. They chewed on the reddish stems during the plague, Russell once told her. It was supposed to ward off evil spirits.

The bus rocked lightly. The windows steamed. The Chinese couple sat across the aisle, hands interlaced like twigs. Ana's eyes slowly closed, then her head drooped sideways. Pars was staring out the window when he felt her hair on his arm, then the weight of her skull drop onto his shoulder. He didn't move. He didn't want to disturb the woman despite the awkward pressure, and the smell of her damp beret.

Outside, a field of salt hay blurred by. A mudflat veined in red. A lagoon. A blue-and-white bird flew up from the reeds and raced alongside the bus. A large beak. A Mohawk. A flash of white wings. Pars saw it—the name in Farsi on the tip of his tongue—and then just as quickly, it was gone.

EIGHT

At Trachis Inn, Kevin arranged fruit in a porcelain bowl. Two apples, a Bosc pear, a banana. The fruit was for Mr. Liang. He'd asked that morning in broken English if he might "inquire" a bowl of fruit for his wife. Not for her to eat, not for *him* to eat, but for their daughter, Tien. They needed to feed her fruit. Food for the dead. Yes, Kevin said, he'd put a bowl in their cottage before they returned. Mr. Liang, bowing up and down, thanked him profusely. He was a small man with thick-framed eyeglasses and liver spots on his forehead. He removed a wallet from his back pocket—he was only being polite—but Kevin blushed and forced him to put it away. Fruit was the least Kevin could afford the dead.

Midmorning, he filled the bowl in the kitchen and set it on the ledge above the sink. The sun brightened through the screens, the green porcelain glowed. A perfect little still life, he thought, with the milky blue sky behind, yet he wished he'd had a pomegranate—only partially for the color. He set aside a peach and an Anjou pear. He'd take those up to the garden himself. His own meager offering to the dead or the yellow jackets, whichever got there first.

He waited until Douglas left for the morning; he didn't want him knowing about the fruit (no doubt he'd have something derisive to say). The bay sparkled outside, the water a glazed blue. The guests were all gone to Caginish; only Sheila Quinn remained down at the cottages, cleaning, changing sheets; her laundry cart sat parked in a patch of sun under the spruces.

Kevin entered the garden. The tomato vines hung with heirlooms, some already rotted on their stalks. The lettuces had just about all bolted. He hadn't had a chance to harvest anything, let alone put up the San Marzanos for winter. He set the fruit on a marble bench at the end of the garden. For the first time in what seemed like weeks, he had a moment to himself. Crows barked in the trees. Hornets buzzed. A yellow butterfly landed on the bench and opened its wings. In the distance, down by the water's edge, three figures in fluorescent blaze vests made a slow sweep along the beach. They were there each midmorning, ground searchers, scouring the shoreline for bits of the plane. Each high tide brought a fresh harvest of shoes and handbags and Styrofoam insulation, and officially all the island beaches were off limits. On the second morning, Kevin had gone with the dog for his morning walk on the strand, only to discover among the eelgrass a windrow of plastic airline cups and drenched clothing. Two gulls were fighting over a bit of something; when he saw a bone attached, his stomach flipped. He grabbed Oscar by the collar and ran back to the house. When the ground searchers arrived later, they sealed whatever it was in an evidence bag. Kevin hadn't been down to the beach since.

He sat now and watched the searchers pick their way along the shore. From up in the garden they looked like figures in an old Flemish painting, gleaners, or sowers of seed, with their walking sticks and nylon sacks slung over shoulders. What was the line of poetry he'd been trying to recall since that night? Something about a painting. Icarus dropping into the sea. The Old Masters. *About suffering they were never wrong . . .* It was Auden, he recalled, but what was the name of the poem?

For the rest of the morning, he cleaned and chopped vegetables, cooked and stewed: a mushroom risotto. A pork shoulder (slathered with garlic, oregano, and salt), an escarole pie (with olives and capers—and anchovies snuck in—for flavor). By one o'clock, the afternoon grew overcast. By two it looked like rain. At three, one of the minibuses gurgled in the driveway. The dog shot out of the house and stood beside the bus, tongue out, tail wagging. Kevin went to greet the guests too. They were climbing off the bus, some with roses in plastic tubes, others with bottles of seawater. The Dutch girl carried a small teddy bear. Everyone's hair looked windswept, disheveled, yet there seemed something slightly different about them now, something that Kevin couldn't put his finger on but noticed nonetheless. They hesitated on the front lawn in clusters and pairs—the Brooklyn family, the woman with the cane—not willing, right away, to return to their rooms. They stretched and lingered. The Italians lit cigarettes. The Dutch girl let Oscar sniff her teddy bear, then tossed it on the lawn and ran after him and played tug-of-war. Mr. and Mrs. Liang headed slowly toward the bluffs.

Some of them would be leaving that evening, returning to the mainland; others had chosen to stay another night—or perhaps longer. Most of their loved ones had not been found yet. Only eleven bodies out of the hundreds thus far had been positively identified. The process was gruelingly slow, given the condition of the bodies they'd recovered (none, actually, intact). Ana Gathreaux, for one, wanted to stay on the island until her husband had been found or at the very least, identified—until she knew he'd actually been on the plane. She had no intention of leaving right away; for what had she to return to? The empty loft, the lab, her Savannah Sparrows? No, she'd stay a few more days. Besides, she hadn't yet visited the hangar at the naval yard at the end of the island. All recovered personal items were being collected and sorted there, and the families had been invited to look among the things.

Pars Mansoor was the last off the minibus. He stepped onto the gravel drive and inhaled the low tide and the privet. The wind had turned warm, somewhat tropical, with spits of rain now and again. He climbed to the portico and nodded at Kevin, who smiled back, and he entered the open double doors into the lobby. The hallway was infused with the odor of pork roast. He passed into the drawing room. He really hadn't paid any attention to the house the night before. It had been dark and he'd spent the day traveling and he'd been interested only in collapsing into a bed—any bed. But now he noticed the green leather couches, the frosted glass globes and brass fixtures, the mahogany table on claw-foot legs. In the dining room, a woman with a frizz of orange hair was setting tables. She blushed when he said hello and returned fixedly to her silverware. He passed through the room and into another off the rear of the house with a billiard table and wooden beads strung on a wire above the baize. A leaded-glass window looked out onto a perennial bed where coneflowers nodded in the breeze. On the green baize sat two balls, one black, one yellow. The eight and the nine. He rolled the yellow gently as he passed.

The night before, when he arrived, Pars had noticed an oddly familiar odor in the house he couldn't quite place. And now, as he wandered through a swing door into the next room, he smelled it again. What was it? Old books! He recognized the odor now: the smell of damp pages beside the sea, that peculiar moldy paper smell. He entered the library—who even knew it was there?—and the odor was exactly the same as that of the library in Remsfjord in Norway, where he'd spent so many hours after he first escaped Iran.

Pars dropped into a red overstuffed chair in the corner. His knees felt slightly weak. He hadn't thought of that town or that library in years. But that particular odor, locked away all this time, brought him back now completely to those long afternoons in the library above the North Sea. And Pars Mansoor had the strangest sensation of having been in that room before. Not necessarily that *exact* room or that *exact* chair, but in the same place, the same state of mind, sixteen years earlier; and for a moment it seemed to Pars that time itself stood still and nothing had changed and he was still that young confused man who'd arrived alone, exiled, friendless, to the small town in Norway.

He sat in the chair with his hands pressed below his chin. Was it something about the room, the books, the North Atlantic light out the windows (mussel blue now); or was it the sudden death of his niece that brought back all those endless autumn afternoons—grief-stricken, alone—when he retreated to the library in Remsfjord? He'd been underground in Tehran for so long, hiding, that it frightened him to walk openly through the streets of Remsfjord, and the library was the only place in town he felt safe, tucked away, hidden among the stacks. No one bothered him there, and he could find a bit of news about Iran in the international papers. The library was the only place he felt remotely at home, among books, even though the books were composed in a completely foreign language.

Pars was the one who'd had to phone his sister in Shiraz. He who had to tell her the news about the crash, who heard, on the other end of the line, the shriek, the silence, the clattering phone, and then his brother-in-law picking up the receiver, saying, "What, what, what?" They'd wept over the phone. They'd howled. And this particular death—so shocking, so out the of blue—brought back all the other deaths of his years of exile: his brother (in the war), his cousin (in jail), his mother (old age), all the other party members of Edalat (assassinated). Each one he'd found out about over the phone, a midnight call from Shiraz or Tehran, the same howling over the trunk line, as if the phone were a conch shell: hollow, oceanic. Hold it up to your ear and hear: despair. He grew to hate the phone those years. Good news always traveled in letters, the bad by phone (for it was too expensive to call the States otherwise). He'd howled too on those nights, while the lights burned across the San Francisco Bay, and he wished he could go back there, if only for an hour, halfway across the world, to Tehran, and now Shiraz, to comfort his sister, to do his duty, to mourn. For he'd been unable to mourn properly all these years for everyone who'd died; unable to do so in public, with his family, at the graveside or in the home of the deceased. Always he was elsewhere, a cruel trick of geography. But returning to Iran meant he might be thrown in jail—or worse. For the last sixteen years, he'd had to meet his family overseas; they couldn't get American visas. So they met once every few years in Berlin or Stockholm or Amsterdam, where they all gathered in a friend's apartment for a week and sat on the floor and wept and laughed and ate the food his mother (now his sister or sisters-in-law) had prepared for days back in Tehran.

Outside the afternoon grew stormy. The windows rattled. A dehumidifier clicked on and hummed. He had to remind himself that things were different now. He wasn't in Remsfjord—despite the spruce forests outside, and the cold blue cast of the sea. He wasn't a bewildered exile. He'd gotten through all that. He'd survived. He'd been married and divorced, had an American passport in his pocket, an apartment in Berkeley, a job in graphic design. His poems had been published in small journals—in both Farsi and English. And yet sitting there, in the library on Trachis, he was thrown into a tailspin, brought back to those terrifying first days of exile.

He closed his eyes and thought of Lailah. Lailah, who was only twenty-four. A bud in the world. The same age he was when he'd fled Iran. She'd come to the United States under a much more benevolent circumstance: a fully paid scholarship in macroeconomics. Was she at all near, Pars wondered, beyond the leaded glass, out on the spit of sand? And lost in these thoughts in the corner of the library, his fingertips grazing his chin, he didn't notice the swing door open, or the figure enter. And neither did Claartija deJong see him sitting in the red chair in the dark. She hadn't been in the library before either; she was just now exploring the house while her brother went down to the beach. She'd come to the library at that very moment, as Pars Mansoor looked up from his trance and saw, silhouetted against the panes of glass, the figure of a young girl.

He felt his spine go cold.

Mrs. Liang passed under the library window just then (she didn't hear Claartija's startled scream). She was picking a bouquet of flowers for her daughter. The sky was unsettled now, the ocean a dark tannin. A few yellow leaves swirled around her. She picked through the perennial bed, snapping stalks of bee balm, spirea, some fall-blooming phlox. With her left hand, she gripped the framed portrait of her daughter; in her right she held the bouquet. The whole flight across the world, she'd held the portrait on her lap. It was a head shot of Tien, taken when she was only seventeen at the photo studio on Chung Shan North Road. Tien looked beautiful in the color photograph, her lips glossed and bee-stung, her eyes dark and shining. She was wearing one of Mrs. Liang's own dresses from the seamstress shop, a taffeta wraparound wedding dress, with tiny pearl buttons that ran in a tight row down the spine. Mrs. Liang was particularly proud of the design; Tien had helped with it too. So simple, so elegant, the legs looked as if they melded together, like a mermaid's. Only a small bit of the dress was visible in the photograph; it showed mostly Tien's face, the high cheekbones; the thin, arched eyebrows; the soft, pale shoulders. Mrs. Liang and her husband often wondered where Tien had gotten her good looks, her height. As young as thirteen, Tien had modeled dresses for Mrs. Liang in the seamstress shop. And it was there where the Hong Kong photographer had found her and left his card, with a Hong Kong address *and* a New York City address. Tien had talent, he told Mrs. Liang;

she had natural looks. She could be a model. She could be in film. He wanted to take some scouting shots. Mrs. Liang was flattered; Tien wasn't so sure (she was just sixteen). The man wore a kind of perfume, and round, black-rimmed, modern glasses and his head was completely shaved. He was renting a studio across town, and he wrote that address as well on the back of one of his cards. Tien was shy, in spite of (or because of) her height. But Mrs. Liang pushed her. When would she have such an opportunity again? A foreigner with an American address. A photographer. Her husband protested: Why fill her head with such dreams? Better she study hard for her exams. But Mrs. Liang got her way in the end—she always did.

Had she not taken Tien the following week to the studio on Chung Shan North Road, things might have turned out differently for Tien. The floors were bare pine in the studio, the ceilings high. There were covers of European magazines framed by the elevator. Girls in exquisite dresses, in bikinis (some nearly naked). A zinc table stood by the entranceway with one pink flower in a green vase. The man's business cards, printed on vellum, lay spread out in a delicate fan.

What happened that day to her daughter on the fifth floor in front of the umbrellas and the Hasselblad and the strobe lights, Mrs. Liang never found out. She'd been left in a separate room. But inside the main loft, flushed from the heat of the lights, the slight chaffing under her arms from the taffeta, and the tightness of the dress around her breasts, Tien felt a little dizzy at first. The photographer was small and encouraging, and he spoke barely any Mandarin. And there was something about the way he moved gently around her, tucked her hair behind her ear, adjusted her limbs, spread out part of her dress, showed her how to pout or hold her chin at just the right angle;

something about his face—smiling, engrossed, responsive—
that allowed her to open up. Perhaps because they didn't speak
the same language; or perhaps it was all the equipment, the
lights, the loft, the electronic music piped softly over speak-
ers, or the many rolls of film and different cameras, all focused
on Tien and Tien alone. By the end of the two hours, she was
laughing with the man from Hong Kong, drinking a bottle of
imported spring water; and she'd let him photograph her in a
way she'd never imagined before, her dress completely loosened
in the back and falling down her shoulders.

So afterward, on the way home, when Mrs. Liang changed
her mind and decided it was wrong, she shouldn't have taken
her daughter, her husband was right (again), it was too late.
Tien had a slight blush on her forehead and perspiration under
her arms. She told her mother nothing despite her endless
queries. Tien was already thinking about the thick, glossy
magazines the man had heaped upon her—the ones he said she
could easily model for—and the vellum card stuck in her
pocket. She certainly didn't tell her mother about how she'd
posed for the photographer, just as, years later, she couldn't tell
her about the other magazines she posed for—and in what
positions.

Mrs. Liang didn't blame herself right away. She was proud
when Tien left home for the first time, despite not finishing
school. Proud when Tien sent the two-page glossy spread from
the American magazine. Tien would call from Hong Kong,
from Hollywood, from Bangkok. Soon she'd settled in a place
called Hoboken in America. Why had she stopped sending
magazine photographs? Mrs. Liang prodded. Tien always
changed the subject (she couldn't send *those* magazines). Why
don't you come visit here in New Jersey? she asked her mother.

Tien could fly them over (she was making plenty of money now). But Mrs. Liang only laughed. What would they do in America, in New Jersey? What would she do with the seamstress shop? No, she told Tien, it's much too far, too complicated. Her husband would hate the journey besides.

Mr. Liang, in fact, would have loved the journey. He'd always dreamed of the American West. He had an unaccountable fondness for John Wayne, and his favorite film was *True Grit* (which in Mandarin he knew as "A Man of Honest Dirt"). But Mrs. Liang put her foot down. She refused to go. It was Tien's duty to come home to see her mother and father. Not the other way around.

The truth was, flying terrified Mrs. Liang. She wouldn't even set foot in a plane. She'd had premonitions yet had told no one. Why hadn't she listened to them more carefully? Why had she made her only daughter fly? How grudging she'd been, how selfish. If only she'd gotten on a plane earlier, her daughter would still be alive. She was more thickheaded than an ox. Hadn't her husband always said so?

In the end, Mrs. Liang had to do what she'd refused to her whole life: she got on a plane. What was the point anymore? She half hoped they'd crash as well, to end her anguish, to get closer to her daughter. She'd boarded the plane at Chiang Kai-Shek International Airport in a paroxysm of tears, her husband and a young stewardess helping her into her seat. She wasn't afraid; all fear had emptied out of her since that night. She felt, instead, in every step, entering the plane, strapping herself to the seat, that she was reliving the last moments of her own daughter's life.

* * *

In the garden, she plucked more flowers. She didn't recognize any of them. They were so unlike the flowers she knew from home. How drab and colorless they were. How parsimonious. But they'd have to do. Would her daughter be satisfied with them? She didn't know; neither did she know if Tien would ever forgive her. She'd been haunted by visions of her daughter ever since arriving on the island, waking dreams of Tien wearing a dress stitched entirely of seaweed and pearls.

Mrs. Liang meandered back to the cottage. The wind blew through her hair, her skin goose-bumped. She was always cold here, on this continent. Ever since she'd arrived in Nova Scotia, the wind seemed to pass right through her.

Back at the cottage, she placed the flowers in a glass of water. Her husband had lit a joss stick on the kitchenette table and sat on the edge of the bed staring into space. It was almost a full week now, the proper time to invite Tien back home. Had they been in their apartment in Taipei, they'd have posted outside their door a large white flag with Tien's name written on it in black ink. They'd have had mourners and incense burning and many bowls of fruit. But that was impossible now. They'd make do with what was on hand: one fruit bowl, a candle, a black Magic Marker borrowed from the innkeeper, a piece of typing paper. Mr. Liang held a white handkerchief with Tien's name crudely inked on it. A bottle of seawater stood beside the framed portrait. It would all have to do. They'd invite Tien here, to this cottage above the Atlantic, for she was still out there in the sea, and they needed to encourage her across the water. The water was the hardest part, Mrs. Liang believed, for the souls of the dead did not like crossing water.

Mr. Liang pulled open the deck door, and the wind gusted inside. Mrs. Liang propped the framed photograph beside the candle and arranged the fruit in front of it.

She looked back at her husband.

Will that do? she asked.

He nodded and said it would.

She took another joss stick from a box and lit it in the candle flame. Then stuck it upright into the flesh of one of the apples. The wind increased outside. A shutter slammed. Was it Tien?

Mrs. Liang shuffled to the edge of the bed and sat and closed her eyes.

Come home, Tien, she began to whisper. Come home with us. Please, Tien, we are here.

Her husband joined her, sitting lightly on the bed; and as he listened to his wife's entreaties, he began slowly echoing the words "Come home, Tien, join us"; first in a choked whisper, then louder, over and over again. Would Tien come? Who knew? (She could be so stubborn—just like her mother.) They'd have to leave the door open and keep pleading with her. They were prepared to call her name all through the night.

Back at the main house, Ana Gathreaux called her brother on Long Island. Her cell phone didn't work—none on Trachis did. So she sat in the antique wooden booth beneath the lobby steps and pulled the louvered door shut, and a bare lightbulb switched on. She dialed and waited for the rings. Her sister-in-law picked up and managed to say all the wrong things before mercifully passing her on to her brother. Ana had nothing in particular to report to Peter, only that she was still there, on the island, and Russell hadn't yet been found. She felt so distant from everyone, especially from those back in New York and her lab—and now from Peter, with whom, in normal times, she had so little in common. She said she'd call in a few days and quickly hung up the receiver before he could ask too many questions.

Afterward, she wandered out to the terrace. The phone call had only made her feel worse. Diana Olmstead, the woman with the cane, was standing at the edge of the lawn, prayer beads wrapped around her wrist. There was a vigil planned for that night, she informed Ana. Mrs. McIntyre had brought candles with paper collars, and they were meeting on the bluff around eight. If she wanted to, if she was up for it, Diana Olmstead said, she should join them.

Ana glanced at the sky.

If, Diana added, it doesn't rain.

Yes, Ana murmured and wrapped her arms tighter against her sweater. But it would rain. She was sure of it. There was every indication in the sky.

NINE

The weather worsened by dark. The candlelight vigil was postponed. The Brooklyn family left on the last ferry, the Hasidic boy and his mother, and the Bulgarian's escort too. Yet the inn remained fairly full, with all but one cottage occupied. Kevin went through the main house, checking doors, sliding storm windows. Trees roared outside; the wind whistled in the eaves. The house felt unsettled. Kevin knew: he'd hardly sleep that night.

By morning, ragged whitecaps tore at the strand. Kevin stood by the window listening in the half-light to the weather band. The computerized voice had been taken off the air, and a real person was reading the forecast: a sure sign that an autumn storm was on its way.

We'll probably lose power, Douglas muttered from the darkened bed.

Yes, Kevin thought, we probably will. He dressed quickly, pulled on socks, and went downstairs. Rain pelted the windows. Someone was sleeping under a blanket on the couch in the drawing room. The Dutch girl, no doubt; he'd found her there the previous morning.

In the kitchen, Sheila Quinn was frying bacon.

Weather looks bad, Mr. Gearns, she said.

Kevin took a mug from the shelf. For two years he'd tried to get Sheila Quinn to call him by his first name; eventually, he just gave up.

He poured himself coffee from a glass pot.

My brother heard that Caginish is all flooded. I'll bet the ferries won't run today.

Probably not, Kevin replied.

Oh, that Red Cross woman's in the office, she pointed with the spatula. She asked to use your phone.

She's here bright and early, Kevin remarked.

Uh-hmm, Sheila said and flipped a strip of bacon in the pan.

Mrs. McIntyre sat at Kevin's desk beside the lamp. She cupped the receiver when he entered.

Sorry, I took the liberties, my cell phone—

I know, Kevin interrupted, it's fine, go ahead.

Thanks, she whispered.

She went back to the phone. He tried not to listen. She was talking about the ferry and the trip to the naval yard. When she hung up, she stood and bit her lip and looked toward the window.

They say the ferries might be canceled.

I know, Kevin said.

We were planning a trip to the naval yard.

You might see how the weather holds. Caginish is flooded.

Does that matter? she asked.

You have to pass it to get there.

I guess it matters.

Kevin sipped from his mug. Rain gusted against the window. Mrs. McIntyre pulled down the hem of her plaid waistcoat. Her hair was perfectly blow-dried.

There's another thing, Kevin said. It's very likely we'll lose power.

Mrs. McIntyre looked alarmed.

He told her that with any kind of bad storm the electricity usually went, sometimes for just a few minutes, other times for several days. The good news, he said, was that the main house had a generator; the bad was, the cottages did not. He just wanted to be prepared in case it should happen. The island's electrical grid was notoriously poor.

We should warn the guests, he added, at the very least.

He took a gulp of coffee and placed the mug in the flat of his hand.

Do you have flashlights? Mrs. McIntyre asked.

Flashlights. Blankets, bottled water, he replied. They had it all, he'd just need some help telling everyone what to do.

She gave him one of her tight smiles.

Just say the word, she said.

You'll be the first to know.

Kevin made a wave of his hand and started back down the hall.

* * *

The rain grew fiercer all morning. Ana Gathreaux stayed inside her cottage. She knew how migrating birds were forced down for days during a storm like this, how they burned up vital body fats they'd stored for their journey—they had only three days' worth to go on—and how they'd need to find food before continuing south. The first-year fledges, who'd never migrated before, often made mistakes in weather such as this, miscalculated landmarks, headed out to sea in front of the storm. Those already migrating over water tried to find shelter wherever they could, on tankers or cargo ships or oil platforms. Thousands crowded on rails or decks, exhausted, panting (and sometimes crews simply swept them into the water). Most birds, however, had to keep flying.

At ten, the minibus failed to arrive at the inn. The ferries had been canceled. There'd be no trip to the naval yard that day. In the main house, Kevin pulled on rubber boots, his Australian riding coat. He'd volunteered to tell the guests in the cottages what to do if the power failed; Mrs. McIntyre would take the rooms in the main house.

Outside, the wind howled. Trees plunged. He could barely keep himself upright against the gale. He fought his way to the Whelk Cottage and banged on the door. There was no answer, but the lights shone inside. He knocked again. Rain sluiced down the oilcloth hood and into his face. Finally, the Bulgarian cracked open the door. He wore a white T-shirt and maroon sweatpants, and it looked as if he'd been sleeping. He left the door open and lumbered back into the room. Kevin stepped inside and shut the door behind. All the lights were burning, and the room smelled powerfully of unwashed clothes.

He began to explain to the Bulgarian that the trip to the

naval yard was canceled and they might lose power. The man stood in the center of the room and appeared only partly aware of Kevin's presence. Kevin wasn't even sure he understood English; he hadn't said a word yet since arriving at the inn. Perhaps he spoke only Bulgarian or Russian or whatever it was he spoke; who knew? If the power goes out, Kevin went on, he should come to the main house. The plumbing won't work here. No electricity, no flushing toilets, no drinking water. But at the house—Kevin pointed—there's a generator, and it will be warm. Everyone else will be there. Okay?

Kevin waited for a response. The Bulgarian simply gazed out the side window. The silence unnerved him, and there was something slightly menacing about the Bulgarian's hulking figure, as if any moment he might smash something—including himself.

Do you understand? Kevin enunciated each vowel.

The Bulgarian lifted his eyes and gave Kevin a barely perceptible, heavy-lidded nod.

Good, Kevin said. He pulled a flashlight from his raincoat and placed it on the table beside the door.

I'm leaving this here, you might need it.

He didn't wait for an acknowledgment. Clearly the man was not coping well. He wondered why his escort had let him stay alone in his condition. He'd have to remember to bring it up with Mrs. McIntyre.

Kevin trudged to the next cottage, and then the next. Everyone else understood well enough and thanked him. The Italians. Ana Gathreaux. The Cliff Cottage was last. He had to talk to the Chinese couple (*Taiwanese,* Mrs. McIntyre had corrected him). He approached the cottage with trepidation. He hadn't seen Mr. or Mrs. Liang all morning. The first day they'd come with a translator, but the translator had slipped away unannounced once they'd gotten settled. The husband at least spoke some English. The cedar steps lay slickened with leaves, the deck door left partly open. The curtains had blown outside and hung plastered against the shingles. Something was obviously amiss. Kevin stamped on the deck to announce himself, shouted hello. It was too dark to see inside the cottage.

Hello! he shouted again.

Mr. Liang appeared in the open deck door, his glasses off, a coat on. He waved Kevin inside. A puddle of water stood by the open door. Why had they left it open? Mr. Liang put a finger to his lips and pointed inside the darkened room.

Sleep, he whispered.

Someone lay in bed, blankets piled on top—Mrs. Liang, Kevin assumed. The room was freezing cold. Apparently they didn't know how to use the thermostat.

The door? Kevin gestured questioningly. Why leave it open?

Mr. Liang slid the glass door partially shut and nodded vigorously.

Ceremony, he said. Ceremony.

He pointed to the kitchenette. On the table two candle ends twitched in front of a framed photograph. Beside it stood the bowl of fruit Kevin had brought the day before, with a stubble of burnt joss sticks sticking out of an apple and a pear. The wind blasted through the deck door. The candles bent and almost blew out, but Mr. Liang seemed intent on keeping the door partly open.

Kevin walked to the thermostat and turned the dial and heard the heater click in the closet.

Heat, Kevin said, and pointed to the thermostat and rubbed his hands together. Warm, he said.

Ah, Mr. Liang nodded. Thank you. Thank you.

Kevin told him about the naval yard and the storm and the generator in the main house. Mr. Liang kept nodding, yet Kevin wasn't sure how much he actually understood. He walked to a light switch and turned on an overhead light.

Electricity, Kevin said and pointed to the light. If it doesn't work, he said, and switched the light off again, come to the big house.

Mr. Liang nodded again and said what sounded like "chintzy" or "intrinsically," but Kevin figured he'd meant electricity.

He handed Mr. Liang a flashlight and waved good-bye. When he left, he made a point of closing the deck door behind.

By noon the rain subsided then returned with a renewed fury. At three o'clock the lights flickered in the kitchen. The radio crackled, and the lights went out altogether. Kevin heard the generator kick on in the cellar. The auxiliary lights glowed in the hallways and the kitchen. He went out to the drawing room. People were coming out of their rooms. The Dutch boy was asking questions. Pars Mansoor appeared in his doorway. Mrs. McIntyre asked what she could do.

Within the hour, all the guests had come up from the cottages. Ana Gathreaux, the Italians, even the Bulgarian; everyone but Mr. and Mrs. Liang. Mrs. McIntyre went to check on them. Meanwhile, Kevin built a fire in the drawing room, and Sheila Quinn brought a tray of sandwiches and quiche—an early, makeshift dinner. Soon the other guests in the main house drifted downstairs. Douglas called—the phone lines still worked—and said he wouldn't be home until very late; they needed him at Government Dock. The search had been called off for the day.

The early evening passed slowly. Some of the guests took coffee in the dining room. Pars and the Italian man set candles in the billiard room and played a round of pool (they couldn't agree on the rules, yet it didn't seem to matter). Diana Olmstead sat with her prayer beads beside the fire. Ana gloomily sipped a cup of bitter tea, listening to the clack of the billiard balls in the other room. Only Mr. and Mrs. Liang stayed in their cottage, lest the ghost of their daughter, who hadn't shown the night before, appear sometime that afternoon.

As the day faded outside, Kevin fed the fire until it blazed in the grate. He brought in candles and set them here and there throughout the drawing room. The generator serviced only the plumbing and refrigeration and a few scattered lights in the house, so the candles were necessary to see by. By seven, just about everyone had gathered around the fireplace. The drawing room was the warmest place in the inn, cozy, with the wind whistling outside and shutters slamming against the old house. Candles flickered on the table and the inn felt like a ship now, rain-tossed, wind-battered. Claartija deJong wandered downstairs, sleepily, wrapped in a cotton blanket, and Diana Olmstead cleared a place for her on the couch.

Diana Olmstead began talking about power outages. As a young woman she'd been caught at Grand Central Station in Manhattan during the famous outage of 1965. Rather than spend the night in the terminal, she'd hiked all the way home to Scarsdale with two other women. They didn't arrive back in the suburbs until after midnight, but it was an experience she'd never forget, three Westchester women hiking through the Bronx along the Grand Concourse. Everyone was so nice along the way! The Italian man said that they thought nothing of power outages in the village where he grew up, that it was more common *not* to have the electricity than to have it. Ana told them that power outages were actually not bad for migrating birds. The grid of lights in the suburbs and the cities—especially the lights of skyscrapers—confused night-flying migrants and often threw them off course or made them crash. Pars Mansoor sat on the couch and listened. In the house in Shiraz where he'd grown up, they'd had electricity but no heat, and on winter nights he and his sisters and brother slept around a brazier filled with burning coals, heads closest to the brazier, bodies radiating out—like petals of a daisy.

Diana Olmstead repositioned her cane by her side. She understood that Ana Gathreaux was an ornithologist. Her first husband had been an avid birder. He used to drag her along on Christmas bird counts in Litchfield County. Once, they'd flown all the way to Costa Rica to see the Lovely Cotingas; that seemed another life to her now, but she still loved watching birds. She turned to Ana and asked what her specialty was.

Migration, Ana said.

So this is normally your busy time of year?

It should be, Ana replied.

I hate to think of migrants on a night like this. Diana Olmstead shuddered and nodded toward the windows.

The Italian woman leaned toward her husband and said something in Italian, and her husband turned to Ana.

Excuse me, he asked. Could you tell us what happens to these birds in the storm like this?

Migrating birds?

Yes, the migrating birds.

The Italian leaned forward on his elbows. Diana Olmstead sat back with her prayer beads in hand. Pars was waiting too.

First of all, Ana started, they don't fly if they know better. Adults usually know better. They find a place to sit out the storm. If the storm is from the south, as they always are this time of year, some birds will fly inland, north and west, to avoid it. Flying inland takes them far off their course, but it's worth the energy expenditure because, well, they have a better chance of survival.

The Italian rested his chin in his hand and lifted two fingers.

Yes, yes, he said, but what about these birds that get catched in . . . He made a circular gesture with his hand, *il uragano*.

A hurricane? Diana Olmstead asked.

Yes, thank you. The Italian nodded and turned back to Ana.

Ana took a sip of cold tea. She'd done a paper on just that subject once as an undergraduate. And she sat back now in the candlelight and told them how a hurricane was a kind of enormous whirlpool, sometimes six hundred miles across, and that migrating birds were sucked into the spiral in a counterclockwise direction—in the north—the way swimmers or scraps of paper were drawn into a strong current. Over the ocean, the eye of a hurricane could be as large as fifty miles wide, and sometimes migrating birds were pulled into the eye itself. Land birds traveling over the ocean got all mixed up with pelagic birds. The thing is, Ana explained, surrounding the eye is a wall of thunderstorms, shoulder to shoulder, and the wall can be as much as five miles thick. The birds who find themselves inside the eye of the storm are in a kind of sanctuary, she said, where the winds can be calm and the sun might be out; but it's an illusion, a vacuum. The ocean below is incredibly violent, with swells as high as fifty feet. Essentially the birds are trapped there inside the eye.

Fascinating, the Italian said.

He interpreted all this for his wife, who listened intently then looked at Ana and nodded.

Diana Olmstead related how once, after a storm, she saw a brown pelican in her pool in northwestern Connecticut. It was amazing how it got there. A pelican! She beamed.

Yes. Ana nodded. All the birds get mixed up and blown off course. That's why, this time of year we get unusual fallouts. People sometimes find exotic species that technically shouldn't be there. It's great for birders, she explained, but bad for the birds.

Pars Mansoor cleared his throat; he'd been silent until now. May I ask, he hesitated, do they find their way back?

Ana turned to him; the others did as well.

Who? she asked.

The ones who get blown off course.

No, Ana shrugged. Not usually. Sometimes they hook up with another flock of a similar species. Cackling Geese with Canada Geese. A Spotted Redshank with a flock of Yellowlegs. They're very forgiving that way, she said. Accidentals occasionally show up from across the Atlantic, British or European birds blown across the sea. They end up on a totally different continent; they seem to survive just fine.

Accidentals? The Italian asked.

Yes—Ana nodded—that's what they call them. The ones who shouldn't be here.

He turned to his wife and interpreted; and she said: *Ah, accidentale, come traviatore.*

Sì. Ana nodded.

Diana Olmstead clapped her hands together. *Traviata!*

Yes, yes, the Italian said. Shall we sing?

They all laughed, a bit mirthlessly, and then sat back in their chairs. Ana thought she'd spoken too much. It was the most she'd said in days. She lifted her teacup; it was too cold to drink, but she brought it to her lips anyhow. Pars seemed somehow unsatisfied. He cleared his throat once more.

What do the accidentals do on their new continent? he asked. What is their . . . role?

That's a good question, Ana said. A question for a behaviorist. It's not really my field. But they can live out a year or so in a flock of a different species, as I understand it. The problem of course is they can't breed.

She gave him a rueful smile. Pars sat back. The Italian woman asked her husband something else, and he turned again to Ana with the question.

If you don't mind, she wants to ask of you: What happens to the birds in the eyes of the storm?

Ana placed her teacup in its saucer. She'd been worried about this question.

Well, she began, tentatively. It's not a pretty picture. The problem is, the birds in the eye really *are* trapped there. They can't fly through the wall of the eye, and they can't land on the water. So they have to keep flying for hours or days, and eventually, they exhaust themselves and drop into the ocean. The ones who get caught in the wall of the eye itself are carried upward on spiraling winds. No one really knows how high these winds go, but it's something incredible, like fifty thousand feet. It's pretty cold, you can imagine, at that altitude. The birds swept up there usually freeze.

And then what? Diana Olmstead asked.

They drop through the atmosphere.

Frozen birds? the Italian said.

Yes. Ana nodded. I'm afraid so.

The Italian pushed his lips out. His wife was batting his leg, asking for the translation. When he told her, she put a hand to her mouth and looked wide-eyed at Ana.

Uccelli agghiacciati? she whispered.

Sì, Ana said, though she wasn't sure exactly what the woman was asking.

Pars closed his eyes and leaned back on the couch. Diana Olmstead unwound her prayer beads from her wrist. They all fell silent. The wind howled. The candles guttered. The Italian stood and stretched his arms behind his back and made a motion to his wife for a cigarette. She handed him the pack from her purse, and then she stood, and they walked together to the dining room for a smoke.

Meanwhile, the night had turned pitch outside and the fire in the grate burned brighter. The darkness in the windows made each of them feel, unconsciously, as if a string had been pulled that drew them all together more tightly than before and cut them off momentarily from the world outside the firelight. Rain drummed on the roof. Ana picked a wool ball off the front of her brown sweater. Pars watched her in the firelight. Her hair had come partially loose from its clip, and she bunched it behind her head and clasped it again. She had long, thin fingers, Pars noticed, but what he couldn't see were the tiny bites in the flesh between the thumb and forefinger of her left hand: the places where her Savannah Sparrows always bit her in the lab.

Kevin walked in just then with an armful of wood and

dropped it by the fireplace. He maneuvered the screen aside, threw a fresh log on the fire, pokered it into position. Everyone watched as orange sparks swirled upward into the flue.

All this time, no one had noticed the Bulgarian moving in the corner of the drawing room. For such a large man, he seemed almost invisible, folded in upon himself, his movements quiet, economical, slow. He carried a brass candelabra he'd taken off one of the sideboards; and with it, he'd wandered around the outskirts of the room, and then into the hallway, and the dining room. The whole house was lit by candles Kevin had meticulously set out. In each room they flickered on tables, against walls, beside windowpanes, just as, a hundred years earlier, the house had been lit by gaslights and candles (and before that, whale blubber). The Bulgarian roamed through the empty dining room, into the billiard room. He was astonished by the effect of the candlelight, for it seemed he'd been transported to another century, another place and time. Who would have thought, weeks earlier, he'd be in a house on an island off North America? Who could have predicted back then, in Sofia, that his wife would be gone forever under the sea?

He went from room to room, his candles dimming and brightening with each step. He pushed through a swing door and entered the library and held the candelabra up to the many books, the many titles. So much paper. So much ink. He brought the flames to the spines of the books and peered at each one as if he were searching for something. Then he came unexpectedly to the piano in the corner of the room and lowered the candelabra. He felt the instrument's top, its sides, its corners, like a blind man fingering the surface of an unknown object.

It was a black-body upright, a Baldwin; he could read the gold-leaf lettering on the front plate above the keyboard. He hinged open the cover and exposed the ivory teeth, and held the candles inches above the keyboard. He hadn't touched a piano since that night over a week ago when he'd gotten the news. Carefully, he pressed the A-flat with one finger. The note was out of tune. He pressed the G. That too. How appropriate, he thought. Like himself. An instrument completely out of whack. He set the candelabra on the wooden top of the piano, pulled out the bench, and laid his entire forehead on the exposed keys. The notes that played—the F-sharp, the G, the B-flat—made a harsh chord, yet no one in the other room heard it: no one had followed him there.

Back in the drawing room, Kevin maneuvered cots into position. The power, he reasoned, wouldn't be restored that night, and there was no point in anyone returning to the darkened cottages or their rooms upstairs with the storm raging outside and no heat or power except on the main floor. It was best for them to stay the night here, beside the fire. There were enough couches and cots, a davenport, a futon, and the bathroom was just down the hall.

Later, he brought more coffee, more cake. There was another game of pool in the billiard room. And now the guests had grown weary. Diana Olmstead yawned and said it was time for her to go to bed. She didn't mind the cold and the dark upstairs. The Dutch boy had already gone to his room with a flashlight. Ana Gathreaux borrowed a pair of flannel pajamas from Kevin. Claartija deJong fell asleep under her blanket in an overstuffed chair. The Italians settled into cots in the dining room. Pars, who couldn't sleep, stayed awake by the fire, writing English words ("accidental," "thrush," "cotinga") into a small spiral notebook.

Who heard the piano first? It might have been Kevin or Ana; or perhaps they heard the notes at precisely the same moment. Kevin thought at first that someone had turned on the stereo in the kitchen but realized that was impossible with the power out. Ana sensed the music came from the library, for she'd seen the Baldwin there the night before. She rose off the davenport and picked her way past slumbering figures, and entered the dining room, where Kevin was listening too. Who dared play music, Kevin wondered, at a time like this? Ana caught Kevin's eye, and the two of them went cautiously down the hall as lightning flashed now and again and lit the walls in a blue, unnatural light.

Ana couldn't tell at first what was being played; but the nearer she drew to the library, the clearer the notes became, until she was sure it was Chopin. A nocturne. She didn't know which one. The music was slow, andante. Her husband liked to listen to Chopin while he worked.

She held the swing door for Kevin. It was too dark to see who was playing, but the notes were clear now, and Ana closed her eyes. Standing there, in the darkened library, she felt a stab of iron enter her heart, as if each chord were a shard of metal, for her husband had listened to that very tune over and over on his stereo in his office, the LP scratched but better—he insisted—than any remastered recording. The nocturnes were the only music Russell could work to. He said they actually helped with his nomenclatural tasks, that listening to Chopin was less like listening to music than like hearing the rain fall on an April night; and shivers ran up Ana's spine as she stood on the rug in the library, for how did the pianist—whoever it was—know about the music, that the first time she and Russell ever made love in his office at the museum, he'd played Chopin? Was it Russell sending a sign? Did he somehow direct this to her? Chopin's nocturne, number 19, in E minor?

Kevin knew the piece of music as well. But for him the moment was partially ruined by the piano. He'd meant so many times to have it tuned. He'd kept after Douglas for months, but Douglas, typically, had done nothing. When they'd first bought the house, they'd had the tuner come from the mainland. But with the moisture and the sea damp (and, frankly, no one playing the thing), it was a losing battle to keep the Baldwin in tune. Still, as he stood there inches away from Ana, Kevin was surprised. With the exception of a few sour notes, the piano really didn't sound that bad.

Neither Kevin nor Ana could make out yet who was playing. The candlelight was too dim to see by, and the player was backlit by a candelabra on top of the piano. Ana stepped closer first, Kevin behind, and they both realized at the same moment: it was the Bulgarian. They exchanged a startled glance and froze in their tracks, afraid that if he felt their presence, if he saw them there, the Bulgarian might stop playing.

In the drawing room, the others heard the faint treble of the piano too—a wavery sound echoing through the halls like music heard underwater. The Italian man woke to it and put a hand on his wife's cheek. Pars heard it too. Claartija roused and sat in tears in the chair (for the notes seemed to massage the place in her left shoulder that had throbbed since the night of the crash). One by one, they rose and with candles and flashlights moved through the house like sleepwalkers feeling their way toward the source of the sound.

When they entered the library, Kevin held a finger to his lips for them to keep quiet, and each in turn put a finger to their mouth as they tiptoed inside the room. The pianist was clearly accomplished, that much was obvious to all. But if what drew them at first to the library was the sound of the nocturne, what kept them there was the realization that the Bulgarian was the musician. He played with his eyes clamped tight, tears moistening his cheeks. And the others listened and wept too, openly or to themselves, for even though the Bulgarian hadn't spoken to any of them the entire time on the island, it seemed that he was the most articulate, the most expressive of them all; that heretofore, his silence had meant more than all their accumulated words combined.

Ana slipped silently out of the room. She could no longer bear the music. Had it been any other tune—Mozart, Jarrett, Monk—she wouldn't have cared. But Chopin . . . *Russell's* Chopin . . . was too much for her to take. Pars watched her go and decided it was best to let her be.

When the nocturne finished, the silence was complete. No one clapped. No one spoke. There were enough candles and flashlights in the room now to see by. Claartija sat on the rug, hugging her knees to her chest. The Italians stood in the corner. The Bulgarian hunched motionless, exhausted, arms hanging at his sides. The rain made a steady tattoo against the windows, and the wind buffeted the leaded panes, yet the storm seemed quieter now, more distant; and the absence of the music felt like the absence of an object or a person that had departed from the room.

The Bulgarian closed the cover to the keys. Ana stepped back through the library door. Her hair was fully down now, wet with rain, her cheeks glistening. No one had seen her before with her hair down, and in the candlelight, she looked to Kevin transformed, younger, quite striking actually. Pars noticed it too. He watched her cross the floor in her flannel pajamas and approach the Bulgarian. She took both his hands in hers (how delicate his were! she thought).

The man's face was clear now, his eyes shining. Ana squeezed his hands. Because she didn't know what else to say, because she wasn't even sure he understood English, she simply whispered, Thank you, thank you.

The Bulgarian bowed stiffly, formally, the way he would in a concert hall; then he strode directly out of the room.

TEN

And so they slept. Each of them wearied by the waiting and then the storm, and now the music, which seemed to cast a spell on them all, inducing sleep. The wind whistled around the house, caught on the eaves, shunted the window glass, made the doors restive in their jambs; but still, they slept. Ana on the davenport, Claartija curled again in the overstuffed chair. The Italians on cots in the dining room, all beneath quilts and comforters. Even the Bulgarian had entered the circle of firelight and lay on the unclaimed couch. Ana handed him a pillow, and he didn't protest but nodded in thanks, then dropped heavily on the velvet-covered cushions.

Wood snapped in the hearth. The Dutch girl snored. The fire slowly fell to embers. Pars didn't return to his room upstairs. He lay instead on a rug on the floor and felt momentarily as if he were back in the safe house in Kurdistan where he'd hidden during his escape from Iran. He and four other refugees—a young Bahá'í boy, a woman from Tehran, the Marxist couple. They'd all slept on kilims on the mud floor for a week, waiting until the new moon, when it was safe to make the crossing at night, on horses whose hoofs were wrapped in felt. Where was the Bahá'í boy now? he wondered. Where was the woman? And because he kept thinking of them, Pars was the only one who couldn't sleep. He lay awake listening to the wind and watching embers breathe in the hearth. The occasional flashes of lightning in the windows were distant now, far out to sea.

Sometime in the night, the rain ceased altogether. The Bulgarian mumbled in his sleep. Ana tossed on the davenport. Pars watched her at one point rise and walk to the window and stare into the night. What was she looking for? he wondered. Her birds? Her husband? On a night like this, it was almost easy to believe they were both out there, trying to get inside.

His mother used to say the soul was a bird that lived in the nape of the neck. At night it flew out of the mouth, and when you woke it returned; and when you died, it flew away forever. The world outside the glass that night seemed entirely an abstraction, a dream. Here, in the drawing room, the living warmed their bones by the flame. Without, the dead were all looking in.

II

ELEVEN

During World War II high-flying pilots over the Atlantic often puzzled over phantom specks that showed up on their radar screens. "Radar angels" they dubbed them and wondered at the faint apparitions, only to learn years later that they were actually birds migrating over open water. Birds, like humans, are mostly moisture—they're ninety percent water—and a flock of finches on a radar screen shows up like a small weather system: one or two green dots. On a night of heavy migration in autumn or spring, a radar screen blossoms with fleeting spectral dots.

There were nights in Manhattan when Ana Gathreaux and her husband sat in front of a computer screen and watched the NEXRAD images of migrating birds. Russell was never terribly interested in what he called Ana's nightly "soap operas," yet he indulged her. Putting aside an issue of *The Auk* or a paper he was preparing, folding his reading glasses, he joined her at the computer. Ana could never resist logging on during a particularly heavy night of migration and staying up watching, sometimes for research, sometimes for pleasure. There was something about the screen, the ghostly images, blooming, fading, appearing, disappearing, that—even after years of watching—still amazed her, to see what had been invisible to ornithologists for years: thousands of birds under cover of darkness, riding the wind like a wave. The seasonal scattering. The radar angels.

When Ana was eight years old, she asked her father where all the birds went in winter. Her father told her—mischievously—that they buried themselves in the bottoms of lakes until the weather grew warm. Little did Frank Gathreaux know he was repeating one of the oldest canards about bird migration, started by Aristotle and believed, amazingly, by Carolus Linnaeus himself: that migratory birds (swallows in particular) hibernated underwater in lakes. For Ana's father, it was merely a convenient lie. They lived a half mile from Lake Ronkonkoma on eastern Long Island, and each afternoon when Frank Gathreaux finished his work at the bakery—exhausted, a cup of coffee in hand—he took Ana and her brother fishing at the lake. Ana wasn't interested in fishing, but she did like birds. Telling his daughter that they hibernated under the water was a way of keeping Ana at the lake. Yet his plan backfired. She wanted to see the hibernating birds for herself.

When do they dive into the water? she asked.

At night.

I want to see.

You can't.

Why not?

They wait until no one is around.

She looked at her father. There was a line of flour dust across his forehead where he'd taken off his baking cap. He sipped from the cardboard cup, a bamboo fishing rod in the other hand. He had the smallest smirk on his face. She crossed her arms; she was determined to see the birds fly into the lake.

I'll wait, she said.

Suit yourself, he shrugged.

He thought it wouldn't last long, a day or two, that she'd grow bored—but he didn't really know his daughter. Each evening for the next two weeks, she went to the lake after supper and waited with a heavy flashlight, a pair of army binoculars, a winter coat, a thermos of hot chocolate (her mother's touch).

Finally, her father had to confess; Ana's mother made him do so.

Frank, she asked one night over dinner. When are you going to tell her?

Soon, soon, he said.

Francis?

Okay. Okay. Her father put down his fork and turned to Ana.

They don't go under the lake, he said.

Who doesn't?

The birds. They don't spend the winter under there. They fly south in winter. They go away.

Ana stopped chewing her food.

I don't believe you, she said.

Her father threw his hands in the air and turned to her mother.

See?

It's your fault, Frank, her mother observed.

He tried again, leaning down to her level at the table.

Honey, I made it up, the stuff about the lake, it's not true.

Daddy lied! Peter shouted.

Peter! her mother scolded.

Ana started eating again. He could say whatever he wanted. This time, she didn't believe him at all.

After dinner, Ana put on her boots again and walked to the lake. Her father joined her as a kind of penance. All that autumn, until December, each evening after dinner, he went with her, with his own thermos of black coffee, his Chesterfields, his coat. In the end, Frank Gathreaux rather enjoyed those twilight vigils with his daughter, waiting for nothing at all, even though he complained about them to her mother at the time.

Decades later, when Ana told friends the story, she added a final twist that Frank Gathreaux would've appreciated: it turned out there *was* a kind of nighthawk, the Common Poorwill (*Phalaenoptilus nuttallii*), that hibernated, half frozen, not at the bottom of a lake but in moist hollows in the high California desert. She found this out in graduate school one night in the library, reading an article in *American Birds*. She'd wanted to tell her father. Did he have any inkling? She'd never know. He'd died years earlier, unexpectedly, a coronary on the golf course on a December afternoon. Ana was nineteen years old at the time. He'd made it to the sixteenth hole.

On Trachis Island, Ana recalled all of this, particularly the afternoons beside the lake, the bronzed oaks, the icy breeze, the smell of his cigarettes. What came back as well was this:

One afternoon she saw a blue and white bird hover and dive into the lake. She stood and shouted to her father: There it is! Something diving into the water. Something hibernating for winter!

A second later, the bird flew up again from the water, a silver fish in its mouth. It was a kingfisher, her father explained; and ever since then the *Alcedinidae,* the kingfishers, became Ana's favorite family of birds.

Why did she recall all of this that night on Trachis Island? Was it the sense of expectancy, of waiting for something that would never show up as she had all those evenings in autumn beside the lake? Was it her father she was thinking about? The odor of his aftershave (Aqua Velva), his red woolen coat, the Chesterfields, the headlights winking across the lake at dusk? Did the loss of her husband bring back that other, original loss, as if one were tied to the other in a lineage of grief, like a country, a latitude, a landscape, she had to visit again? It was more than a week now since Ana had heard the news, and nothing had become any easier.

There was one other thing Ana recalled from that autumn on Lake Ronkonkoma years ago. One night her father looked up the word "migration" in *The Book of Knowledge*; they had the full set in the basement of their house. He wanted to prove to Ana at last that birds indeed did fly south in winter, and didn't hibernate under lakes. She couldn't recall what the chapter said about bird migration, or even *if* there was a chapter on bird migration. But she did remember him reading a definition of "migration." "Migration," from the Latin *migratus,* he'd read. To remove, to leave, to abandon one region for another.

* * *

The storm surge passed early that morning. The winds abated; the sky grew calm. The day broke chilly and brilliant. Kevin brought his coffee out to the stone terrace. Leaves and branches lay scattered across the lawn. The beach below looked rearranged, with a fresh shelf of sand spat up from the storm. The electricity had hummed back on sometime in the early morning.

In the kitchen, he took out a sack of potatoes, a bag of onions, a carton of eggs. Sheila Quinn had called earlier. Her basement had flooded, and she couldn't make it in. Kevin had told her not to worry; he'd deal with breakfast and the room cleaning himself. He hoped he'd see her that evening.

He set skillets now on the stove, a pot of water to boil potatoes. Sunlight slanted through the windows. The Dutch girl wandered in, rings beneath her eyes. She was still draped in the cotton blanket she'd worn the night before.

Good morning, Kevin said.

She shrugged and plopped herself on one of the stools beside the counter.

What makes it so good? she asked.

Kevin ignored the question. He was scrubbing potatoes at the sink.

Did you sleep last night?

I slept.

On the couch?

The chair.

Is your room okay?

She yawned and laid a hand over her mouth. The blanket slipped from her back and exposed a bare shoulder; she was wearing a sleeveless T. There was some kind of tattoo on her left biceps.

The room's fine, she said, it's my brother who's a drag.

I'm sorry, he replied.

Yeah. So am I.

She planted her elbows on the table, a fist on each cheek, and watched Kevin.

It made him a bit uneasy. Teenage girls as a rule made him tense. He'd spent so little time around them that they seemed an entirely different species. This one, with the dyed hair and the eyebrow ring, seemed particularly farouche.

He pointed with the scrub brush to her arm.

What's the tattoo? he asked.

She pulled down the blanket. He wasn't sure if he was seeing correctly.

Groene eieren met ham, she said.

He peered closer at her white shoulder.

Green eggs and ham, she translated.

Oh. You're a fan of Dr. Seuss?

She pushed out her lips.

Not especially, she shrugged. I thought it was cool.

I see.

He went back to the potatoes.

Can I ask you something? she said. Do you like living here?

In this house?

On this island. Doesn't it get boring?

A little. Yes. I like boring.

I think I'd go *nuts,* she said.

You very well might.

He lit the stove under a skillet and knifed a large gob of butter into the pan.

She lifted her face off her fists.

Can I do something? she asked.

Like?

Help, she said.

It's okay. He shook his head.

No, really. I want to.

She stood and threw the blanket over her left shoulder like a serape. He looked around at the scrubbed potatoes, the bag of onions, the eggs.

Well, if you really . . .

Yes. She nodded.

Well . . . potatoes or onions, pick your poison.

Hmmm. Onions, she decided.

Kevin raised an eyebrow. Ambitious, he said.

He walked around the counter, set a Lucite cutting board in front of her, and handed her a chef's knife by the handle.

It's very sharp, he warned. So be careful.

I'm not an idiot, she scowled.

He placed five large yellow onions on the cutting board.

Okay, medium-size pieces, please.

What are we making? she asked.

Home fries.

She'd never heard of them. He told her what they were. The sun glowed through the windows. She pushed hair behind her ear and started cutting. Kevin went back to the sink. He tried not to watch but couldn't stop himself. The blanket kept slipping off her shoulders, and she was doing it all wrong, cutting the onions before even peeling the skin. He bit his tongue; she was going to cut herself; he was sure of it. He had to say *something*. He wiped his hands on his apron and came around the counter.

Here, he said, let me show you.

I can do it.

I know you can, but there's a trick I learned years ago.

He gestured for the knife, and she handed it back reluctantly, then stood beside him with a hand on her hip.

First you slice off the ends. It's a round object, and you want it to be stable, and the ends you don't eat anyhow.

He cut off the bottom and the top of the onion and flicked the discards aside with the back of the knife.

Then you want to peel the skin, like this.

He made a small slit down the length of the onion and slid the outside layer off with a finger, then sliced the onion in half and set the two naked hemispheres flat on the board.

Now it's stable and you can do anything to it.

Anything?

He looked at her; she was smirking.

You know what I mean.

Okay, okay, she said impatiently and motioned for the knife.

He handed it back, the handle toward her, and returned to the stove.

They worked side by side for a while in silence, Kevin glancing up every now and then to monitor her. He put the potatoes on to parboil. Cracked eggs in a bowl. Chopped green pepper. The blanket fell off her shoulders again.

Can I get you a sweater? he suggested.

I'm fine, she said.

You sure?

I'm *fine*. She glared.

He let it go. She was biting her bottom lip in concentration, sniffling back tears, wiping her nose on her forearm.

You can do it in front of running water, that sometimes helps, he offered.

She didn't answer. He let her be. He wondered about her brother, her parents. He asked where in Holland she was from. She told him the south, near Belgium, in the town where Philips built the first lightbulb. He said he didn't know where that was, and she drew the shape of Holland on the top of the cutting board with the tip of the knife.

Right there. She pressed at the spot. We live there.

Oh, Kevin said, and resisted telling her not to press the point of the blade into the board.

Claartija wiped her nose again and went back to the onions. The potatoes were simmering in the pot. Douglas walked in freshly shaved and dressed in a clean polo shirt. He'd returned early that morning.

Hello, he said.

Claartija greeted him with a wave of the knife. He poured a mug of coffee for himself and blew on the porcelain. He shot Kevin a questioning look, and Kevin shrugged in return.

I see you've been enlisted, Douglas said to Claartija.

I volunteered.

Onions no less.

Her choice, Kevin remarked.

What are you making?

House fries, Claartija said.

Home fries, Kevin corrected.

Whatever, she muttered.

Douglas looked at Kevin. Why don't you get her a sweater?

She prefers the blanket, Kevin said.

Claartija rolled her eyes.

Douglas shook his head and left the room. A minute later

he returned with a mustard-colored cardigan and set it on the stool beside her.

Here, he said, it's better than that blanket.

She looked at the sweater.

Ach, she made a face. I can't wear that.

We'll find you something more fashionable later. He held it up with two hands. Go on, he urged.

She shook her head but put the knife down anyhow and allowed him to slip the sweater up her bare arms. Kevin watched in amazement, surprised she'd let him—but even more astonished at Douglas.

The sweater was much too large. Claartija waited impatiently while Douglas rolled each sleeve to the wrist. Kevin watched from across the room and felt all at once—unexpectedly—a pang of jealousy. Was it the attention Douglas was paying the girl, or the ease with which he acted around her? He couldn't tell, but seeing them together in the sunlight, he felt the slightest bit . . . left out.

Douglas stepped back and inspected the girl.

Not bad. He made an appraising face.

It's awful, Claartija protested and muttered something in Dutch. Then they both turned to Kevin at the same moment.

Kevin felt his face go hot. He picked up a skillet and turned to the stove. Claartija sighed and took the knife back to her onions. When Kevin regained his composure, he glanced over at the girl. She was sniffling again, and the yellow sweater really didn't look so bad. Douglas, leaning against the fridge, wore the tiniest smirk of satisfaction across his face.

TWELVE

By eight that morning the recovery operation resumed again. Sea King helicopters thudded across the waters. Naval ships appeared once more offshore. The divers went down, the ROVs, searching again for the black box, the flight data recorder, for thus far only the voice recorder had been found. In a hangar on the mainland, workers fit together recovered bits of the fuselage on a giant jig. All over the island, ground searchers started their rounds once more. If anyone had entertained hopes of a lone survivor before, the storm dashed any such speculation: for nothing could have survived such a gale, such waves. The storm spread wreckage in a fan shape one hundred miles from the crash, and evidence had been pulverized into a fine particulum. Calls came now from eighty miles down the coast, where someone had found an airplane meal washed ashore, the molded entrée plate completely intact: beef bourguignon and a flowered carrot still perfect in its plastic wrap.

* * *

At Trachis Inn, the guests returned to their cottages to shower, change, pack. The Italians left just after breakfast. Claartija's brother too. He'd been planning on leaving for days. There was nothing left for him on the island, and he'd never really wanted to come in the first place. It was Claartija's idea; she'd insisted they go not just to Nova Scotia but to Trachis Island itself. Her brother, however, couldn't care less. Once their parents' bodies had been identified the first day, he'd wanted to head home. He was interested only in the lawsuit, and the whole time on the island he'd jotted notes, made lists, written down what the airline representatives said (and what they didn't say), for who knew, it might be important for the lawsuit—especially if they said something stupid. His early morning phone calls to Amsterdam, to New York City, his interviews with lawyers maddened Claartija, for it seemed so heartless—his way of grieving. How different the two of them were. Seven years separated them, but it may as well have been decades. Claartija always suspected one of them—probably she—was an adopted child.

She watched her brother shoulder his aluminum briefcase and climb into the back of a waiting limousine. She felt a momentary pang of anxiety; he was, after all, her only brother. But she'd made her decision the day before to stay on the island. She wasn't ready to leave yet, and the airline would fly her back whenever she wanted. There was nothing he could say about it now.

Diana Olmstead caned out to the driveway to wave goodbye to those leaving. Kevin came out too. Afterward, Diana Olmstead put an arm around Claartija's shoulder and gave it a gentle squeeze. Mrs. McIntyre padded over on sneakers and held out an offering to Claartija: an open tin of Altoids. Wintergreen.

At noon, the minibus returned. The remaining guests were heading to the naval yard at last. Ana sat on one side of the bus, Pars on the other. Mrs. McIntyre counted heads. Half the seats lay empty. On the Peninsular Road, the wind scattered leaves; the sky was Wedgwood blue, the trees changing orange and red. It was autumn already, Ana thought wistfully, peering out the window. For days she'd been dreading this trip to the hangar. Others had been there already, picking through the possessions of the dead. She wasn't sure which she feared most: finding something of Russell's, or finding nothing at all.

They drove past fields of grazing Jerseys. Meadows gone to seed. Late herons like lawn statues in estuaries. At the end of the island, they arrived at a gate. Quonset huts shimmered under the afternoon sun. Dozens of vehicles sat parked on a weedy tarmac. An airplane hangar glittered beside the sea.

It took a moment for Ana to adjust to the fluorescent lights inside. Men in white jumpsuits and orange gloves moved about the hangar, some on foot, some steering forklifts. A man in a blue suit and bushy sideburns addressed them all. The personal possessions, he said, were still technically evidence, but the families were welcome to look among them and identify things that had belonged to their loved ones. He instructed them not to touch anything but to call over one of the technicians posted at each table. The items themselves were separated by category: handbags on one table, overcoats on another, laptops and brief-cases on another, and so on. They could have the personal pos-

sessions back, he said, but not right away. They needed to fill
out some forms, and the items would be returned to their
rightful owners as soon as possible.

He pressed his palms together in front of his chest.

Are there any questions?

No one had any questions. Mrs. Liang started moving
toward the tables. The man held his clipboard out to the side
and said, okay, they were free to wander at will.

Ana headed toward the back. She wanted to start in one corner and work her way systematically toward the front. The
tables were draped with white cloth, the items numbered with
index cards, some secured in plastic bags with recovery tags
attached. Men and women stood stationed at a respectful distance between every few tables, gloved hands behind their
backs. The hangar was hushed, sepulchral, yet the tables
looked disturbingly familiar, like those at a church tag sale, or
a down-at-the-heels department store. Women's purses sat side
by side, handbags with leather straps, rhinestones, a Coach
bag, a Gucci. Ana had to remind herself to keep focused; she
felt her forehead go damp with sweat.

She stopped at a table filled with footwear. There must have
been over eighty individual shoes—pumps, espadrilles, Birken-
stocks, cowboy boots—some in pairs, others alone. Russell was
a loafer man. Bass Weejuns his favorites, with beef rolls or
sometimes tassels (he was particular about his shoes). Ana's
heart raced when she saw a loafer, but it was much too large for
Russell's. A size eleven at least—and it was black; he *never*
bought black, always oxblood or brown. She circled the table
twice, her heart still thudding, until she was certain: Russell's
shoes were definitely not there.

She moved on to the next table where Pars stood frozen,

staring at dozens of watches laid neatly in rows: wristwatches with thin gold bands, digital displays. A Bart Simpson watch. A New York Yankees watch. Ana touched his elbow.

Are you all right? she asked.

No. He shook his head, then said: They're still ticking.

Ana leaned closer. She hadn't noticed it at first. The glass was still intact on most of them. All of the second hands were jerking together in syncopation.

Jesus, she whispered.

Pars checked his own wristwatch. All of them, he saw, were set correctly to Eastern standard time.

The Bulgarian man walked past at that moment but didn't stop at the watches. His wife never wore one; it got in the way of her playing. He stopped instead at a table of eyewear. He scanned the dozens of sunglasses and bifocals and horn-rims. In the last two years, Evdokiya had started wearing reading glasses when studying notation. She was self-conscious about them at first and wore them only inside their flat in Sofia, but then slowly she brought them into the world. Secretly, they thrilled Orfeo Raskolov. He found them rather sexy. He'd even bought her a pair of pearl-rimmed cat's-eye glasses just that summer, yet she refused to wear them. She preferred the cheap throwaways she found on racks in European discount stores.

Orfeo saw neither the cheap discount nor the cat's-eye glasses on the table. Yet glancing up, he spied, leaning against a wall two aisles away—half-hidden behind a suitcase—something that made his heart stop: a blue cello case.

Just then a shriek came from across the hangar (Orfeo

Raskolov paid it little mind). Mrs. Liang had spotted her daughter's tiny black backpack on one of the tables, and she'd nearly fainted against her husband's shoulder. The backpack was no bigger than a loaf of bread and Mrs. Liang would recognize it anywhere: the black leather, the spaghetti straps, the brass clasps. Tien had worn it the last time she came home to Taipei, and Mrs. Liang had puzzled over the size. So absurdly small. So impractical. Why would anyone wear such a ludicrous thing? Fashion, Tien said; it was not about what you *put* in it. What kind of fashion was that? Mrs. Liang wondered aloud, though secretly, she admired the Italian leather.

Now, she rushed toward the backpack and snatched it off the table. One of the men in white suits tried to intervene. Did she recognize the backpack? he asked. Would she like to fill out a form? But Mrs. Liang ignored him. The leather was still damp. She tore open the clasps and emptied the bag's contents on the table. Tien's things were still inside! A compact disc player, her lip gloss! A prescription bottle. Even her passport!

The technician in the white suit was explaining—as gently as possible—that she wasn't supposed to take anything. But Mrs. Liang was hysterical now, and her husband was trying to calm her. The technician kept intervening until the supervisor in the blue suit rushed over and took the technician aside. It was okay, he said. Leave her be. Mrs. Liang, meanwhile, clutched the bag to her chest. She wasn't going to let it out of her sight. Not this time. She'd rushed to the next table, searching frantically for anything else that belonged to Tien.

* * *

The blue cello case was without a doubt Evdokiya's. They'd bought the pricey thermoplastic case together in Paris. Orfeo Raskolov was drawn to it now almost in a trance, slightly trembling, for she'd loved that cello. It was one of a kind. A Guadagnini with a rich, sonorous tone, a beautiful amber varnish, a small nick in the bottom center of the back. She'd even given her a name (it *was* a she, Evdokiya insisted): Chanterelle. "Chanti" for short.

Orfeo approached the cello cautiously. He had to move a black suitcase aside to reach it. In no other time since arriving on Trachis did Evdokiya feel so close, so near, and he stood before the case a moment, his whole body shivering, and touched the shiny plastic, the metal clasps. One was snapped off, and the plastic had been scratched. He ran a hand along the gentle hump of the case, unhinged the other clasps. He was afraid to open it, afraid of what he'd find, the plates smashed or shattered, and his heart thumped loudly in his throat. He was surprised the case had been found in the first place, but when he swung open the cover, what he saw surprised him even more: there was no instrument inside.

He closed his eyes and ran a hand over the pelt of red velvet. It was only slightly damp, still soft to the touch. What had become of the cello? He opened the pocket inside the case and found a used cake of rosin and a G string coiled in a circle.

Ana, who'd been watching the Bulgarian from across the room, walked over and stood behind him. He was running his hands over the entire inside of the case. When he opened his eyes again, Ana stepped toward him.

Is it hers? she asked.

He nodded yes.

She plays the cello, Ana said beneath her breath, almost to herself.

A man in a white jumpsuit and orange gloves approached and stood attentively a few feet behind. He wore a blue visor cap with the initials CTSB on it.

Orfeo turned to him at last.

Has the cello been found? he asked. Or any parts of it?

It was the first full sentence Ana had heard the Bulgarian speak. The man in the jumpsuit shook his head.

No, sir, I don't believe so. But—he held up one hand—wait here, please.

He disappeared somewhere into the back. Ana waited beside Orfeo. They didn't speak. Orfeo stared into the velvet of the case as if he were peering into a pool. The case looked to Ana like the inside of a wisteria pod, the hard shell so surprisingly soft inside, the seed gone. A door opened somewhere in the back and flooded the hangar momentarily in a golden afternoon light. Then it shut again, and the man in the jumpsuit returned carrying a small plastic bag and handed it to Orfeo.

This is all, he said, so far.

There were numbers, coordinates, written in black ink on the clear plastic. Orfeo unsealed the top of the bag and shook its contents into his palm.

A cello bridge has two arched feet that rest on top of the instrument and a heart-shaped hole carved in its center. The thin piece of maple provides the ideal medium for sound: it carries wire strings on its back and transfers their vibration into the body of the instrument—and music comes out the other end. All this Orfeo knew from his earliest years of musical instruction. But the bridge he held in his hand now seemed almost an alien object. The heart shape surprised him; he'd never really thought about it before; and the wood felt so light, so flimsy, yet apparently indestructible.

Orfeo closed his palm over the wood; it fit perfectly in his hand. He brought the bridge to his face and inhaled the maple, then turned to the man in the jumpsuit.

May I keep it? he asked.

The man in the jumpsuit held a finger in the air.

One second, he said and disappeared again.

He returned a moment later with a clipboard and handed it to the Bulgarian.

Where are you staying? he asked.

Orfeo turned to Ana.

Trachis Inn, she answered.

We can return it to you there in two days. Or we can send it to your home later.

Orfeo placed the bridge lovingly back in its plastic bag, sealed the top, and handed it across to the man.

I will wait for it, he said, at the inn.

Outside, in the sharp afternoon light, Pars Mansoor smoked a cigarette in the parking lot. He'd found his niece's passport; he'd found her carry-on bag (the label was still attached). He'd even found a few thousand Iranian toomans—the notes already dried and vacuum-sealed in plastic. He'd filled out all the appropriate forms. The money and everything else would be flown back home to her family in Shiraz, the supervisor promised, as soon as it had been examined, cleared, and logged in to a computer.

THIRTEEN

Late afternoon the bus returned to the inn. Ana entered the main house feeling worse than she had in days. She'd found nothing of Russell's at the hangar, only a blue Mont Blanc pen that might—or might not—have been his. What had become of his leather satchel? she wondered. His luggage? His passport? Not to mention the man himself. They'd found nothing of him yet. How could he have just simply disappeared?

The sun was dropping through trees outside. She walked through the empty lobby. The rooms seemed desolate now with so many guests gone. The housecleaner was vacuuming the hallway. There was a noticeable chill in the air. Perhaps it was time, Ana thought, to return home. But what was there for her back in New York City? An empty loft, her lab, her life—what *used* to be her life. However awful things were on the island, it couldn't be as bad as returning home with nothing to show for herself, or Russell's self. As long as she stayed on Trachis Island, her life remained suspended in a kind of solution, where there seemed to her an illogical glimmer of hope—for what or whom, she wasn't quite sure. At the very least, she wanted a piece of Russell, some evidence, a patch of clothing or a positive ID. A tube of deoxyribonucleic acid that would at least confirm he'd been on the plane.

She entered the library. The last of the day lingered in the windows. How long had she been on the island? Three days? Four? Was it more? It seemed she'd endured there for weeks.

She stood among the books and the dust motes in the empty room. What was it about the library that gave her the smallest drop of comfort? She kept returning there each evening. The room reminded her somehow of Russell; at least he would've appreciated the library, the crowd of armchairs, the green glass shades, the fake Tiffany lamps. The books on papyrology, Norse gods, salt mining. An entire shelf housed Greek literature in translation: Herodotus, Pythagoras, the Epicureans (each book dog-eared and Kevin Gearns's name penned on the inside cover). Russell would have liked that too, and the oak shelves which smelled of lemon furniture wax.

She picked out an old volume of Jean-Henri Fabre's *Life of the Caterpillar*. The pages looked as if they'd been steeped in tea. The book was one of Russell's favorites—he'd grown up with it in England—and seeing the title, taking it off the shelf, brushing dust from the leather cover, Ana felt a peculiar tingle, as she had the night before with the Chopin. Why, of all books, should she find that *here*?

The first time she'd met Russell was at the American Museum of Natural History in New York City. Ana was a new intern in the Ornithology Department, Russell the assistant to the collections manager. In the main lobby, Ana waited anxiously on a bench under the enormous barasaurus, and Russell was the one who came down to fetch her. On the elevator, he gently quizzed her about her work. He had a slight Oxbridge accent, a supercilious grin. He wore brown loafers—Weejuns, of course—and no socks.

He gave her a tour that day of the department, the systematics lab, the ABA Prism sequencer that analyzed the DNA of dead birds. But only downstairs, in the vast, quiet crypt where they kept the collection of bird skins, sealed in cabinets, did he become fully animated. He recited numbers (850,000 study skins, the largest collection in the world). He pulled open cabinets, rolled out aluminum drawers, showed her shelf after shelf of birds, all laid out like iridescent items in a jeweler's shop. There were twenty per drawer, still colorful, beaks all angled to the left, cotton plugs in place of eyeballs. They were so beautiful and fastidiously arranged Ana was almost afraid to touch them.

May I? she asked.

Be my guest, he said.

She gently picked up a skin, untwisted the yellowed tag attached to its leg. River Kingfisher, it read. *Alcedo atthis*. 1908. It was captured along the Cam River. Cambridgeshire, UK. The study skin weighed next to nothing, a paper doll; the stiff blue feathers smelled vaguely of naphthalene—musty, mothballish, not unpleasant. It reminded Ana of her grandparents' apartment.

Russell stood staring at the bird in Ana's hand.

"Thus lovely halcyons dive into the main, Then show far off their shining plumes again."

She looked at him.

Shakespeare?

He shook his head.

Longfellow?

He made a disapproving face.

She handed him back the skin.

I give up.

William Cowper.

I would've never gotten that, she conceded.

You like coraciiforms? he asked.

Yes, in fact they were her favorite order. The family of king-fishers in particular. The punks of the avian world, with their harsh cackle, their outsize beaks, their attitude, the Mohawk.

And of course, Russell added, the story attached to them—all, sadly, untrue.

Uh-hmm, Ana said absently.

Russell laid the skin carefully back in its drawer. A portrait of Lord Rothschild stared down at them from the wall. They continued on that afternoon to the Chapman Memorial Hall of North American Birds, and then the rest of the museum. Months later, he made love to her under the same portrait of Rothschild, at night, pressed against one of the cold steel cabinets, with his sockless loafers, her bare foot on the back of his calf. Russell had keys to all the rooms; and at night, when everyone but the night watchmen had gone home, they roamed the tiled halls like teenagers, mischievously making love in the Chapman Hall, beside the Fuertes mural of flamingos or the dioramas of Peregrines on the cliffs of the Palisades (using the wooden banister for purchase) or the glass case of North American raptors. They copulated in the lab too, beside the humming DNA sequencer. Russell wanted to have sex in each room (it *is* a museum of natural history after all, he argued). They tried it in the Pickling Room as well, with its odor of formalde-hyde, its shelves of glass jars filled with birds in alcohol—pickled puffins and grebes.

That was where Ana drew the line.

The smell is revolting, she said, buttoning her blouse.

Arousing, he whispered. He licked her neck and put two fingers on her chin. I find it complex, like . . . a Merlot.

She pulled away.

Enough, she said and went to the sink and washed. A glossy ibis stared from one of the jars, light glowing through the liquid.

No one will ever accuse *you* of being a romantic, she said.

He was buttoning his shirt. He had a gleam in his eye.

I'll take you to dinner, he offered.

I've lost my appetite.

Soon Ana put an end to their after-hours activities. She was sure they'd get caught. She was only an intern still. But more than that, the collection rooms felt slightly possessed, with all those dead birds from centuries past sealed inside eight-foot steel cabinets. Even during the day when she walked through them, the rooms remained half-lit and deserted, the marble eyes of owls and godwits staring from old glass cases. One could hear the echoes of museum goers on the other side of the thick concrete walls. Out there, in the halls of the museum, the public wandered completely unaware of the rooms hidden inside the heart of the museum—where nearly a million birds lay entombed. That was the strangest part, the laughter and noise that came from behind the walls. She always felt as if she were walking inside a crypt.

All of that seemed so many years ago to Ana, when Russell had seduced her with stories about early bird collectors, men who'd died from arsenical soap or in the bush or fallen from cliffs while collecting swallow nests. Some shot or murdered in the far reaches of the globe, there only to capture an unknown bird species. He too had the fever. He explained it as a mania for going out and gathering in the world. Was it not a way of showing one's love for everything out there? he maintained. A strange way to show it, Ana quipped, by killing it.

When she first met Russell, they used to go spring mornings to see the migrants in Central Park. A foggy morning after a warm front—or an abrupt shift from southerly to northerly winds—brought a fallout of birds on any given May morning: thousands of migrants pinned down for the day in the Ramble or along the lake. On the way home, in the streets, they'd find dozens of dazed or injured (or more likely dead) birds. Drawn by the lights the night before, the migrants found themselves in the morning trapped in the canyons of Manhattan. They'd be attracted to the lush planters on ground-floor lobbies of office buildings, and—not knowing better—they'd fly into the glass trying to get to the tropical greenery. Ana brought paper bags to pick up the dazed birds (Zabar's or Macy's for woodpeckers, brown sandwich bags for warblers). Back in the loft, she'd rehabilitate the injured ones and release them days later up in Inwood Hill Park, where they could fly unhindered to the north. Russell called it sentimental, her rehabilitating the birds. And she stopped doing it after their marriage. She hadn't the time anymore or the inclination, and New York City Audubon volunteers patrolled the streets now in the mornings during migration. But she remembered those first days with Russell as some of the happiest in her unmarried life, the way they'd crawl back into bed unshowered, with the loft door open, just as the rest of the world was waking, and they pleasantly weary from their miles of walking in the dawn.

Sometimes she was surprised they'd lasted as a couple, not just for a year or two but fifteen now, both of them growing into their lives like fingers fitting gloves. Russell had been made the head of the collection and went to conferences around the world. And she had published papers on migration and *zugunruhe,* and biogenic magnetite in the brains of migrating Savannah Sparrows. There was a time when they'd tried (halfheartedly, without success) to have children. But that had passed. And after a sense of failure and defeat, they had recovered and a new feeling emerged, a deepening that drew them closer in ways subtle and profound—both tied more to their work than before. They bought a plot of land in upstate New York and camped there some weekends, in a green nylon tent, dreaming of the house they were in no rush to build and one day retire in. True, Russell was often gone, traveling, and she was often lost in her own labwork; and their attentions to each other had attenuated to a comfortable neglect; yet they were not unhappy. Russell was a cushion, something solid to press against. Was that not love? Predictability, knowing where each of them would be. A GPS reading. A way of orienting through the turbulence of the world? Their life went on, unthoughtful, unmindful, until that morning the call came, and she thought, Russell, my Russell. Why had she not known where he'd be?

Something now about the library on Trachis Island reminded Ana of the collection rooms, the smell of fumigants, the waxed floors. Books, birds—both of them preserved. In the collection rooms, the living rubbed against the dead all the time, all those birds entombed inside aluminum drawers like seeds or husks dried long ago; and in the old library, the books were like that too, with foxed pages inside cardboard covers. Was it this that gave her the smallest sand grain of solace? The dark wood? The leaded-glass windows, the upright piano in the corner?

Russell told her one night after making love in the empty halls of the museum that if you listened carefully, you could hear all the dead birds in their display cases communing with each other.

What does it sound like? Ana asked.

Esperanto, he replied. Only for avifauna.

I see, she said.

Actually, it's a kind of low humming.

He'd tried to look serious, but he was joking, of course. And yet Russell did, on one occasion, confess to believing in ghosts. Not the Esperanto-speaking kind, or stuffed animals in glass cases speaking with their syringes. But real ones. Real ghosts.

You're not serious? Ana had asked, raising one eyebrow.

Well—Russell nodded—if you must know, I am.

She'd laughed at him. How could a biologist believe in ghosts? He couldn't answer; he just did. Ana shook her head. Not she. She wouldn't hear of it. And yet, standing in the library just then, with the book open and the sun dropping into the sea, she wasn't sure that if he was there she'd laugh at him anymore.

FOURTEEN

Early the next morning, Mrs. McIntyre rushed into the kitchen, out of breath, hair uncombed. Kevin was just pouring coffee into his mug.

Have you seen Mrs. Liang? she asked.

No, Kevin said.

She glanced nervously around the kitchen, darted to the back door, and peered through the screen. Kevin set the coffeepot down.

I think we have a situation. She turned to Kevin. Her husband can't find her.

Did he look in the garden? Kevin suggested. Sometimes I've seen her there.

The garden, the beach. Apparently he's looked everywhere. Mrs. McIntyre exhaled. He woke up this morning and she was gone.

Kevin rinsed his hands and wiped them on a towel.

Please—she started from the room—would you come with me?

Of course, Kevin replied and followed her into the hall.

Mr. Liang sat crumpled in a chair in the dining room. He was speaking hurriedly in bits of broken English and Mandarin. Diana Olmstead sat beside him, one hand on his forearm, cane between her legs. Mr. Liang was relating the story he'd already told Mrs. McIntyre: How he'd woken that morning and his wife was gone along with the framed photograph of their daughter and her little black backpack. He'd headed down to the beach to look for her because some mornings she went there. He found her slippers about a quarter mile from the cottage, near the water's edge, but no Mrs. Liang.

He reached beneath the chair and brought up a pair of sand-encrusted slippers to show them.

It's okay, dear, Diana Olmstead whispered and patted Mr. Liang's arm. I'm sure we'll find her.

He put the slippers back down, removed his glasses, and wiped his red eyes. He said he'd taken something the night before to help him sleep, and now he blamed himself. He should have been more careful. He lowered his head into both hands, and his shoulders began shaking.

Claartija wandered into the room, blanket over her back, and looked at Kevin.

What happened? she whispered.

Mr. Liang's wife is missing.

Oh great. Claartija rolled her eyes.

Have you seen her?

Me?

She can't be far, Diana Olmstead announced. Perhaps she went for a longer walk than usual.

She glanced over Mr. Liang's head at Kevin.

Why don't I look around the house? Kevin suggested.

Claartija offered to help.

Diana, Mrs. McIntyre said and gestured to the man. Would you . . .

Yes, dear, I'll stay with him.

Thank you. I need to make some phone calls.

Mrs. McIntyre left the room and hurried to the office. In all her ten years as a disaster counselor, this was the call she'd dreaded most: one of her charges lost, one of them gone AWOL—or worse—under her watch. It was Mrs. McIntyre's job after all to prevent such a thing. She'd been so focused on the Bulgarian, who was alone and hadn't uttered a word for days, that she'd lost sight of Mrs. Liang, who at least had her husband with her.

Heretofore she'd been so careful. She'd attended workshops, seminars, lectures on bereavement and grief management and post-traumatic stress disorder. She'd helped on nearly a dozen other disasters. The suitcase in her rented car had six pantsuits, all slate gray (somber, modest, though not funereal); four pairs of shoes (hiking boots if needed, sneakers, and two pairs of sensible pumps); two silk scarves (for her neck); extra boxes of tissues, aspirin, eyeglasses, underwear and socks and a case of bottled water (specifically for the families). Yet despite the hours on the ground, her professionalism, she'd failed. Perhaps she should have called for more psychiatric help on the island; perhaps the translator should have stayed longer.

She dialed her supervisor's number. He'd contact the RCMP, the airline, whatever other officials needed calling. She'd waste no time now. They *needed* to find Mrs. Liang.

Within thirty minutes the news spread to the remaining guests, and all of them joined the search. Pars Mansoor hiked the south end of the beach, Ana Gathreaux took the north. Kevin rechecked all the rooms and the cellar, and drove with Claartija deJong along the Peninsular Road; perhaps she'd wandered out to the highway. Meanwhile, a squad car arrived with the RCMP investigator and the island constable, Bunty Phillips. The investigator debriefed Mrs. McIntyre first, then Mr. Liang and all the other guests. They were sending a helicopter; they were sending ground searchers. A Taiwanese social worker was flying in from Toronto.

Before he left, the investigator took Mrs. McIntyre aside in the hallway and removed his hat.

This isn't your fault, you know, he said.

She appreciated the words; he had to say them. He was toying uncomfortably with the brim of his hat. Yet nothing he said could help.

Two hours later, Pars returned from the beach with Ana. They were red-faced, windswept. Ana was limping; she'd stepped on a piece of driftwood, and a splinter had lodged in her foot. The tide was up, Ana explained, which might've covered any footprints from earlier that day. They'd seen nothing. They'd done their best. The police were taking over the search. All they could do now was wait.

* * *

Pars went back to his room on the second floor. If he'd planned on leaving that day, he'd changed his mind. He couldn't depart in the middle of the crisis over Mrs. Liang. Besides, he was concerned about Ana. She seemed so alone, so vulnerable. Suffering seemed so new to her—as it did, he often thought, to most Americans. Sometimes he saw spasms of anger flicker across her face followed by looks of utter anguish. While the death of his niece was a terrible shock, he hadn't actually seen the girl in sixteen years; yet for Ana he felt a great encompassing sympathy for the loss of her husband, and he wanted to make sure she'd be all right.

Diana Olmstead helped Mr. Liang back to his cottage and brewed him a cup of valerian tea for his nerves. She sat with him in the light of the open deck door, steam swirling from their cups. Mr. Liang chewed on his lower lip while Diana Olmstead fingered her prayer beads. Even before that morning she'd planned on staying at Trachis Inn. She felt it her duty, not just for her sister—whose body was one of the first to be identified—but for the souls of all the dead who still lingered over the water. For forty-nine days, they'd remain close, in the liminal state, the *bardo* state—confused and agitated; and it was her duty as a Buddhist (converted, yes) to help guide them through this terrifying time. The dead needed comfort, as did the living. They needed prayer. They needed to be read the Sutra for the Intermediate State. So each morning, Diana Olmstead caned her way to the beach and perched on a boulder with her prayer beads and the tiny rice-paper book with Tibetan script inside. She could understand only bits of the writing from her yearlong retreat in Dharamsala, but the words themselves didn't matter so much as the sound of them. So what if she mispronounced a few sentences and forgot whole parts? It was the act that mattered most, and the practice of *Né Dren,* guiding the souls of the dead through their transmigration. She believed it all helped, her prayers, her presence, the beads. A sutra was a thread, a cord, and a prayer as well. She liked the word "sutra" and the idea of threading something together that had been ripped apart. A torn fabric. Suturing the souls of the dead back into the cloth of their new bodies.

Now, with Mrs. Liang missing, Diana Olmstead had a whole new purpose for staying on Trachis aside from tending to the dead. She needed to watch Mr. Liang. He was resting now in a chaise longue opposite her, his eyes closed. She repositioned her chair so the sun fell on her face. The poor man, she thought, first his daughter, now his wife missing. She inhaled deeply the smell of ocean. She started her prayers, reciting silently to herself, making sure to focus. She believed, based on nothing but her own intuition, that his wife, at least, would be found.

The day turned warm. The afternoon came slowly. Of all the remaining guests, Orfeo Raskolov alone knew nothing about Mrs. Liang's disappearance. He'd stayed inside his cottage and emerged only in the late afternoon. No one seemed to be around. The lawn lay empty, the beach too. He slipped up to the main house but saw no one there either, and the library was desolate as well. He pulled out the piano bench and sat. Someone had left a window open, and he could hear the sound of the surf below. He touched the keys, as he had two nights earlier, and played again, this time Beethoven: the *Pathétique.* Sonata number 8 in C minor. He closed his eyes. He could almost see the music, the shape of the notes within the first few measures.

He played the chords with abandon. He didn't care if anyone came in, as they had the other night. What would Orfeo Raskolov tell them if he had words instead of octaves? Would he tell them about his wife: how she was one of his students at the State Academy of Music in Sofia? How she'd come to class early one afternoon in the rehearsal room on Evlogy Georgiev Street. Orfeo Raskolov once played the cello himself—but had since given it up for the piano. And that afternoon in the rehearsal room, Evdokiya asked for help with her bowing. When she couldn't get the angle right, he stood behind her and held her elbows outward, two fingers firmly supporting the ulna of each arm. Relax, he told her. Breathe, he told her. Don't tighten your shoulders. She couldn't relax at first; she felt like a marionette. But eventually she did, and as he held her elbows at her sides, she began moving her right arm fluidly, back and forth, while he kept reminding her to breathe.

That afternoon Evdokiya wore a white linen shirt, a black pleated skirt. Her hair was wrapped in a bun. Orfeo was married at the time, Evdokiya engaged. Orfeo hadn't meant to be so forward in the rehearsal hall; he'd have helped any one of his students with the same technique. But unlike the others, she distracted him that afternoon as he lifted her arms perpendicularly in the air. Her hair smelled of grass and cigarette smoke from the Number 4 bus she'd taken across the city—and there were freckles on the back of her neck, inches from his face. Cars honked out on Georgiev Street; the summer afternoon had grown hot. She sat with her back erect, perspiring, the heel of the cello nestled between her breasts. He could smell the deodorant under her arms.

When Orfeo stepped away from her, she kept her elbows held in the air, as if they were suspended by invisible strings.

Then suddenly, self-consciously, she giggled and blushed and said: Just like a puppet! The light was coming in through the high clerestory windows; some other students had entered the room, talking to each other, setting up stands. Had she felt it too? He didn't want to know. He was her professor; she was twenty years younger.

What else might he tell the others? How he'd left his wife and four children; how she'd run away from her fiancé. How scandalous it was at the time. He was chastised; she, shunned. He was a lech; she, an opportunist. But then, as the years passed, and they accompanied each other in concerts, and her abilities grew (and eventually outshone his own), they were mostly forgiven. It was meant to be, people said. It was love. How could it be helped? Yet his children and his ex-wife wouldn't speak to him, and hadn't in eleven years.

In their flat outside Sofia, Evdokiya practiced in the late afternoons. Orfeo liked to listen and coach her while he cooked dinner or read a book. What do you think of that G natural? he'd ask. Could the scherzo be pluckier? What of the pace? Sometimes while she was playing, he approached her from behind and touched the tip of her right elbow as a reminder, not of her bowing but of that afternoon. She still wore her hair in a bun, but her bowing was seamless now, beautiful to watch. Other times, he'd rest his palm lightly in the middle of her back, just below the two points of her shoulder blades. He liked to feel the musculature beneath her dress, the thoracic muscles tightening and loosening with each pass of the bow. It felt to him like a bird learning to fly.

The last concert they performed together was Haydn's *Farewell* Symphony—ironically enough. She'd continued with her career, touring now with the Bulgarian Philharmonic. She was to meet them in Amsterdam for a concert of Richard Strauss's *Metamorphoses.*

Orfeo told no one any of this. Instead, he poured himself into the piano. What was the point of speaking? When you play a cello, your whole body vibrates with the wood. You open your legs and let the instrument resonate up your body, through the lumbar and into the rib cage. That was the thing Orfeo Raskolov missed most about not playing the cello; and that was what he had told Evdokiya that afternoon in the rehearsal room eleven years ago: how, to play the instrument correctly, you had to let yourself be a conduit, the wick of a flame. *You* had to resonate, as well as the instrument. And that was what he'd felt that summer afternoon in the rehearsal hall: both of them resonating together, at the same time, as if they were one string spanned on the same wooden box.

He played the Beethoven. It was his favorite sonata, the silences, the gentle phrasing. Still, he missed the cello. When you bowed a cello string, you created not one sound but a whole set of overtones, each of which—together—created the illusion, the sensation of a single note.

FIFTEEN

By nightfall, Mrs. Liang hadn't been found. At the main house, Kevin put out dinner—French onion soup, chicken *à la piémontaise,* a frisée salad—but no one had an appetite. Afterward, in the Quahog Cottage, Ana couldn't sleep. The splinter in her foot pulsed. She counted waves. Sixteen per minute. She turned all the lights on in the cottage, ransacked the cabinets for tweezers. Even if she found a pair, she probably couldn't reach the damn thing; it was right on the outstep of her left heel. Finally, she pulled on jeans and headed to the main house.

A few lights were burning in the upstairs rooms, but the place seemed abandoned. The ocean boomed below. The television flickered with the sound off in the drawing room. In the library she found Pars on all fours, examining something on the carpet.

I'm sorry, she said and turned to go.

It's quite all right. He gestured her in, then stood and colored. She gave him a quizzical look.

You were having a moment, she said.

It was nothing . . . momentous. It's the rug. He slipped his glasses on.

It's from Isfahan, he explained. I was just checking the cartouche. My grandfather used to deal in wool. Actually, it's a pretty good weave.

Really?

Uh-hmm . . . Many, many knots.

Oh, Ana said.

She looked around the room as if expecting someone. They were both silent a moment. Ana toyed absently with the ring on her left hand.

Pars brightened. Oh, I forgot. I have something for you.

He went to the shelves, searched the books, then pulled one down and walked back to her.

What is it?

Go ahead.

She looked at the cover: *The Conference of Birds* by Farid ud-Din Attar. She opened the first page.

I thought you might be interested because—he shrugged—the birds.

She laughed drily.

Well, it's not exactly ornithological, he said. But the main character is, what do you call it . . . a hopi.

Hoopoe, she corrected. A coraciiform.

He gave her a questioning look. She waved a hand dismissively.

It's nothing, she muttered. Just taxonomy.

Oh, he said. Anyhow. The Attar is a Sufi story, an allegory.

You might find it, I don't know . . . amusing. I'm not familiar with this translation, however, and Attar is not the real master.

Who's the real master?

Pars's face lit up.

Hafiz.

He gestured to the bookcases. Alas, he said, there is no Hafiz.

She thanked him and closed the cover of the book. They could hear the ocean outside. Ana laid a hand on her neck and looked uneasily toward the open windows.

Are you okay? he asked.

I think I need a drink.

Mrs. Liang?

Everything. She shrugged.

I saw a bottle of gin on the kitchen table, he said and raised an eyebrow.

We can attempt a martini, Ana said.

I wouldn't know how, he confessed.

We'll need vermouth to start. And olives.

I'm not very good at drinks, he admitted.

I can see that. Come—she waved—there's got to be vermouth somewhere in the house.

She tucked the book in her back pocket, and Pars followed her out of the library. They went through the darkened halls. The lamps were out in the dining room. She found the switch in the kitchen and flooded the room with overhead light. A bottle of Gilbey's sat alone on the stainless-steel counter.

Should we ask Kevin? Pars inquired.

He's probably asleep, Ana said. I'm sure we can find some vermouth.

She checked the shelves by the stove. Cooking wines, sherry. Olive oil. She went into the pantry and searched among large vinegar bottles, fish sauce, sacks of sugar.

Maybe we should look at the bar, Pars suggested from the other room.

Ana peeked her head around the corner.

Why didn't I think of that?

I don't know, he said.

Several minutes later they both sat at a wrought-iron table on the stone terrace. Pars brought a bucket of ice, the gin bottle. Ana a glass shaker and two martini glasses and a bottle of Noilly Prat. Pars lit a candle in a glass flue on the table. The moon had risen in the east, a tiny fingernail clip. The wind was light. They could hear buoy bells banging gently somewhere out at sea. Ana mixed the drinks. She'd learned how from Russell. A martini, he liked to say, was merely a vehicle for the olive. Sevillanas preferably. Two or more. He liked his dirty, with a splash of olive juice. But Ana hadn't found any olives at the bar, and that seemed appropriate too. The gin and vermouth would have to do on their own.

She handed Pars a glass and apologized and said it should really be colder and it should really have at least one olive, but—did it matter?

No. He shook his head decisively and lifted the glass in the direction of the ocean. She lifted hers too. Ana sipped. Pars made a face and put his glass down.

It's that bad?

No, he said. It's . . . interesting.

Sorry. Perhaps we should have skipped the vermouth altogether.

It's fine, he protested, and took another tentative sip.

155

Ana closed her eyes. The breeze smelled of low tide. The dog had wandered over from the lawn and stood beside her, wagging his tail. He laid his head on the armrest of her chair and looked up at her.

He likes you, Pars observed.

He likes getting rubbed.

The dog sat, and she scratched his head behind the ears and then his chest.

He's been visiting my cottage, she explained.

Do you know what he is?

A Portuguese water dog.

When she stopped scratching, the dog lifted his right paw and set it on top of her forearm.

Enough, she said and raised her drink again.

The dog tilted his head at her, then looked at Pars.

Enough, Oscar, Ana said. Go lie down.

You know his name?

Kevin told me.

The dog clicked away, circled, and lay down at the edge of the terrace, and looked out into the night. Ana slipped off her sandals, cradled her left foot in her crotch, and tried to pick at the splinter. Pars nodded toward her foot.

It's still there?

Yes.

He put his drink down.

Here, let me see. He gestured toward her foot.

It's fine, she said.

Come on, I went to medical school. I'm practically a specialist.

In splinters?

He scooted his chair closer and brought the candle to the

156

edge of the table. He reached into his trouser pocket and pulled out a Swiss Army knife.

You're prepared, she said.

Yes. A real Boy Scout.

He pulled out a miniature tweezers from the end of the knife.

May I tell you a story about a splinter? he asked. Actually it's about a stone. It's a very old Persian story. Everyone in Iran knows a version of the patient stone. My mother used to tell it to me.

Sure. Ana shrugged.

Pars removed the glass flue from the candle and held the tweezers to the flame, one side, then the other, sterilizing the metal.

There was, he started, a very poor girl who stopped at a big castle one day for water. She was thirsty and a long way from home. As soon as she entered the courtyard of the castle, a gate slammed shut and she couldn't get out. In the middle of the courtyard lay a sleeping prince whose back was bloody and covered with a thousand thorns. Beside him was a note that read: Whoever removes the last thorn from my back shall be my bride.

Pars set the glass flue back on its base. Ana had drawn her knees up to her chin and sat listening in her chair.

The poor girl was dressed in rags, Pars continued. She wasn't interested in marrying the prince; that was beyond her imagination. But as the hours went by, and she couldn't leave the castle, she began picking thorns out of the prince's back, one after the other. At first it was merely something to pass the time, but soon it became a challenge. One day passed, then another, and each day she removed a few more thorns. It was difficult work. But after several weeks, she began actually to like this prince, even though they'd not spoken a word to each other.

At last the day came when only one thorn was left in the prince's back. The poor girl in rags was about to pull the last thorn out when a woman in a gold dress burst into the courtyard, pushed the girl aside, and snatched the last thorn from the prince's back.

At that very moment the prince awoke and saw the girl in rags—she'd fallen to the ground—and the woman in the gold dress holding the thorn triumphantly over his head.

"Prince," the woman in gold said. "I've taken all the thorns from your back, and here is the last one as proof."

"Then you shall be my bride," the prince announced.

The girl in rags lay on the ground still. She was not used to talking to princes, so she said nothing.

The woman in the gold dress said, "Prince, I'll marry you only if you make this ragged girl my slave."

"So be it," the Prince declared. And so it was.

Pars lifted his martini and took a cautious sip.

Not a very cheery story, Ana commented.

Wait, it doesn't end there.

He put the glass on the table; there was a slight mischievous look on his face.

One day, he continued, the prince was going to the city and asked the poor slave girl if he could bring something back for her.

"A stone," she said. "There's a purple stone by the bank of the river under a big casuarina tree. Please bring it back for me."

"What for?" the prince asked.

"I cannot tell," the poor girl said.

This piqued the prince's curiosity, but he asked nothing more.

When he returned the next day with the stone, the poor girl set it beside her bed in the slave quarters. Each night she told the stone her sorrows. She told the stone about her poor parents and how she had to go out and beg for food; she told the stone about how she'd come to the castle for a cup of water, and how she'd removed all thousand thorns from the prince's back, and how the woman in the gold dress took advantage of her at the very last moment. Each night, she told the stone the same story over and over, and each night she told it, the stone grew bigger. Every time she recounted the story, the stone took on a bit of the weight of her grief and grew heavier, until after many weeks, the small stone was the size of a tremendous boulder!

The prince, meanwhile, had grown curious about this stone. How come it kept getting larger? So one night he hid behind the door of her room and listened while she poured out her grief to the stone. When she came to the end, he burst into the room and said: "Poor girl, what you say must be true, because the stone keeps growing with your story. And so I have betrayed you. It is *you* I should have married." And with that, he banished the woman in the gold dress from the castle and made the poor girl in rags his bride.

Is that it? Ana asked.

Pars took a sip from his drink.

More or less, he shrugged.

What about the stone?

Pars smiled slyly. He removed his glasses and began cleaning the lenses with the tail of his shirt.

Everyone has a patient stone, Pars explained. You see, my mother used to tell that story, and I believed it. You tell your story enough times, and you leave a bit of it behind, some of the misery rubs off with each telling.

Do you still believe it?

I don't know, Pars said. It's a very Persian idea, telling stories to survive, weaving them into a fabric. Do you know about Shahrazade?

A little, Ana said.

She was actually Iranian. Not everyone knows that. They assume the Arabian Tales are Arab, but in fact the *Hazar Afsana* was originally Persian.

Ana sighed and unfolded her arms.

But I forgot something, Pars said.

What?

He nodded toward her foot. Your splinter.

Oh, that.

He set his glasses back on the bridge of his nose and gestured for her leg. She laid her foot on his knee, and he brought the candle close to see by. His forehead gleamed in the candlelight. The tendon on the left side of his neck tightened. She could smell his warm, ginny breath. She closed her eyes. The pain was not so bad. When she opened them again, he was holding the tweezers up to the light.

Here's the culprit.

He unscrewed the bottle of gin and poured a capful on the skin of her foot where the splinter had been.

Very professional. She made a face. I'm impressed.

I was almost a surgeon, he said. Honest to God.

She poured him another drink and filled her own glass as well.

Why "almost"? she asked.

That's a long story.

He leaned back in his chair and took a pack of cigarettes from his jacket. Do you mind? he asked.

Please, she said.

He lit one and exhaled. He told her how he'd studied to be a doctor in Tehran, but then the revolution came; and afterward, he was arrested because of his activities in the Socialist party. He told her about his months underground, about escaping Iran through the mountains, about his year in Norway and coming after to the United States.

Why didn't you get a degree here? she asked.

Pars exhaled a long seam of smoke.

It was too much money, he shrugged. And too much time gone by. I needed a job besides. And really no one wanted an Iranian surgeon at the time.

He smiled ruefully and tapped ash on the terrace, and they both fell silent. She was tempted to add, They still probably don't, but she kept silent.

The moon had risen and drifted in a thin geography of clouds. The dog let out a low growl and sniffed the air.

What about Mrs. Liang? Ana finally said.

What about *Mr.* Liang? Pars replied and picked a piece of tobacco from his lip.

It's a very tough thing, you know, Pars said philosophically. But so is the heart. When I was very young, my mother handed me a knife in the kitchen. She was cutting up a chicken for dinner. Parviz, she said, take this, and she gave me the knife in one hand and put something slimy into my other hand. It was the chicken's heart, the—what do you call it?—giblets. She wanted me to cut it. Go ahead, she said. Have you ever tried to cut a chicken heart? It's a very tough muscle. She wanted to show me that. I couldn't cut the damn thing!

Maybe the knife was dull, Ana suggested.

Pars smiled and raised his cigarette.

Yes, I never thought of that.

They fell silent again. Ana drained her glass. She felt a bit light-headed. She mixed another shaker full of gin and vermouth and added ice. The dog stood and began barking at the bluffs. He looked back at them, then barked again.

What is it, Oscar? she asked.

His tail was erect now, and he barked more insistently.

What do you think it is? Pars asked.

A rabbit? A deer?

They both looked at each other and had the same thought at once: Mrs. Liang.

Maybe we should just check, Pars said. He tamped out his cigarette and stood.

Ana picked up the shaker and stepped into her sandals.

The lawn was already wet with the night. They followed the dog toward the bluffs. The wind kept pulsing from the sea. They took the steep cedar steps down to the beach, Ana gripping the banister in one hand, the shaker in the other.

The tide was far out, the flats thinly glazed with moonlight. Oscar loped to the water's edge. He wasn't barking anymore. They scanned up and down the beach, but saw nothing, only the sand faintly lit in the night.

False alarm? Ana asked. Maybe it *was* a rabbit.

Who knows? Pars shrugged. He stretched his arms overhead.

Ana handed him the shaker and he took a gulp, and she did too, then nestled the glass in the sand. She wanted to feel the water. She kicked off her sandals and rolled her jeans to her ankles.

You're not going in, are you? he asked.

She'd already started toward the water.

Just a little, she shouted.

Because, Pars said, I can't . . . but his voice was snatched by the breeze.

The water lay before her, a silver curtain, diaphanous in the moonlight. Her feet touched the foam. Ice on her toes. Her ankles. A wave splashed her jeans. What was it like out there on a night like this? she wondered. She closed her eyes. The wind felt warm but the water deadly. She went deeper. There were little sparkles on the surface, a blue luminescence. Plant life talking to each other. She thought of Russell and almost broke into sobs. She heard Pars shouting behind.

She turned and trudged back up the strand. He was standing at the water's edge, legs apart, shoes in hand. He hadn't gone any closer.

What did you say? she asked, holding her hair back.

I can't swim, he confessed.

You're joking.

He looked at her impishly. His glasses were off.

I'm not.

Come on. She grabbed his arm.

Stop.

Oh, come on, just feel the water on your feet.

She dragged him down the strand. He only half protested. His face scrunched when the water hit his ankles.

That's far enough, he said. The bottoms of their pants were getting wet. She didn't care. She liked the tug of the undertow around her heels, the tide coaxing her out.

Afterward, back on the shore, they found the shaker and sat in the sand. The stars swirled lightly overhead. She pointed out Cassiopeia. She told him that birds could navigate by certain constellations, that the young learned "sky maps" by watching stars rotate around the North Pole. He told her about the stars over Kurdistan, the brightest he'd ever seen. She took a sip from the tumbler. The ice had melted, and the drink tasted pretty awful by now.

I think I need some water, Ana said.

No more, Pars pleaded.

Fresh water, she said. A drink.

She stood and brushed sand off her elbows and held a hand out to him.

They wandered back up the steps. The dog followed them to her cottage and lay down outside on the deck. Ana found a towel. There was sand inside her jeans. Pars was hesitant to enter.

I don't want to ruin the carpet, he said.

Oh, come on, it's just sand.

When he went to reach for the lamp, she shouted: Don't!

Sorry.

I can't take the lights.

Okay, he said. No lights.

Thank you.

She left her sandals by the door and poured two large glasses of water and handed him one and they drank.

She felt light-headed from the gin, the late hour, the salt water. The sand was cold on her feet. She took the clip from the back of her head and shook her hair loose.

I'll be right back, she announced. There're some crackers or something in the cabinet, if you want.

I'm fine, Pars said.

She went into the bathroom and changed out of her jeans into the only other thing she'd brought, a long print dress.

When she came back out, Pars was sitting on the edge of the couch. She settled beside him. They didn't speak for a long time. Pars finally put down his glass and sighed.

I should go, he said. It's late.

Without thinking, Ana lifted her hand to the left side of his neck and pressed her fingers into the tight tendon she'd seen earlier.

What's this? she asked.

I don't know. He groaned. It's very painful.

No kidding.

She pressed into the tissue, and he let out a little yelp.

Relax, she whispered.

He turned away and closed his eyes. She closed hers too. Russell had good hands. He'd taught her about the muscles, each one labeled with its own Latin.

She ran her thumb down Pars's jugular.

God that hurts, he moaned.

It's the Terrible Triangle, she explained—all this vascular stuff.

She pressed her thumb into the hollow above his collarbone.

How do you know this? he murmured.

Anatomy classes, she said.

Right.

Shhh, she whispered.

He grunted, removed his glasses, and closed his eyes.

The deck door lay open. The sea breeze nosed inside. Ana could hear chimes somewhere in the night.

Here, let me do this properly.

She moved some pillows aside and made a place for him on the couch to lie down. He hesitated, and she told him to relax, it was only a massage.

Within twenty minutes, Pars lay on the couch, gently snoring on his side. Ana stood and went to the kitchen and poured another glass of water. She'd wanted oblivion; she dimly realized that now, if only for a few hours. But she was, unfortunately, completely sober.

She went to the door, slid it partly shut. Leaves clattered in the wind outside. The dog was gone from the deck. Back at the couch, she covered Pars with a white sheet and stood over him a moment, listening to his breath. Maybe this was stupid, she thought, but she didn't care. She could still hear the ocean seething outside, like a third party, insistent, demanding. On subzero nights in the North Country, kinglets huddled together on branches. Did anyone blame them for sharing their warmth to survive? She pulled up the sheet and laid beside Pars on the couch, her back to him. Then she lifted his outer arm over her shoulder and draped it carefully across her chest.

SIXTEEN

A heavy dew fell in the night. Kevin woke at dawn. A little before seven he heard tires crunching on gravel and wondered who it could be, arriving so early in the morning.

He went outside with his mug of coffee. The lawn glistened in the cold. A squad car idled in the drive, blue exhaust drifting upward. Bunty Phillips slowly climbed from the car and put one hand on the roof. Kevin would recognize him anywhere—the burly figure, the red muttonchops, the fishing cap. He was the island's part-time constable—and full-time fisherman. He'd never spoken more than three words to Kevin or Douglas until the day before.

Good morning Mr. Gearns, he said

Good morning. Kevin lifted his mug. Would you care for some hot coffee? I've just made a pot.

Bunty waved his hand. No thanks. I've got some news about your missing guest.

Kevin braced himself. The radio crackled inside the car.

They found her, Bunty said.

Is she all right?

Just a bit confused and a little chilled, I'd say.

Kevin closed his eyes. Thank god, he murmured.

She was at the Trachis Lighthouse, Bunty explained. She must have walked there in low tide and gotten inside the building. They found her upstairs in the lantern house. She was talking a blue streak. Someone with his head on had the good sense to look up there. Her husband will be relieved anyhow, Bunty added.

Everyone will be, Kevin said.

Bunty told him that she was down at Trachis Harbor with the EMS. That Mrs. McIntyre was on her way to pick up the husband.

You might want to break the news first, he suggested.

Kevin nodded. Bunty looked over the roof of the car out toward the gray ocean. Kevin did the same, and they stood a moment staring together on the drive. Static erupted on the car radio.

Oh, there's another thing, nearly forgot.

Bunty leaned into the car, grabbed something off the dash, and raised himself again.

This is for one of your guests. I told the RCMP man I'd bring it here. Name's on it.

Kevin thanked him and took the clear plastic bag.

You sure you don't want to come in? he offered. Breakfast will be ready in a few minutes.

Can't, Bunty said. I appreciate the offer.

He banged the roof of the car and lowered himself into the driver's seat. There was a time, at a public meeting years before, when Bunty Phillips had used Kevin and Douglas as examples of the new people coming to ruin the island. But Kevin had the oddest urge right then to hug him.

He watched Bunty put the vehicle in gear and lift a finger in parting. Bunty Phillips. He couldn't wait to tell Douglas they'd talked, that he seemed *actually okay* after all this time.

When the squad car was gone, Kevin stood in the driveway. The leaves had begun dropping from the pin oaks. Fog lay on the lawn. Kevin had almost forgotten about the plastic bag, and he looked down at it now in his hands. "Orfeo Raskolov" was written on a white label and "Trachis Inn" scribbled beneath it. Inside he could make out the rectangle of wood, but out of context, without the body of the instrument, it took Kevin a moment to realize what it was. The wood was the size of an index card, with two feet on the bottom and a hole in the center in the shape of a heart. He put the bag to his chest. What a gift, he thought, looking out over the lawn, to be handed such a thing: a bridge, a span, from Bunty (of all people) to pass on to the Bulgarian. Kevin stood a moment in the gray dawn. A shiver ran up his spine. He had good news for Mr. Liang—for everyone—and a piece of cello for the Bulgarian.

Down at the Quahog Cottage, Pars Mansoor covered Ana with a proper blanket from the bed and brewed coffee. He tiptoed out to the deck and stood in the chilled air. He didn't want to wake Ana: she was sleeping so peacefully inside.

At the Cliff Cottage, Diana Olmstead sat on her deck as well—eyes half shut, reciting her sutra. She'd spent the night keeping vigil over Mr. Liang. He hadn't slept at all. Only in the last two hours had he finally fallen asleep.

On the second floor of the main house, Claartija deJong slept too. She dreamt of her parents and her brother; and in her vivid dream all of them were together in a car, driving through a tunnel in the Alps.

Orfeo Raskolov was the only one else awake. He'd gotten up with the dawn and was just now strolling along the path toward the main house. The first sun of the day fanned weakly through oyster clouds. A crow cawed somewhere overhead. He saw Kevin walking toward him on the path, a plastic bag in hand. The sun shone on the clear plastic, and Orfeo Raskolov knew immediately what the bag contained.

And so they all left Trachis Inn that day. First Mr. Liang went with Mrs. McIntyre to join his wife in Trachis Harbor. Then Orfeo Raskolov, who'd packed his bags that morning and took a taxi to the noon ferry. From there he was flying home to Sofia. Ana Gathreaux decided to leave as well that morning. There was no avoiding her life anymore. So what if they'd found nothing of Russell's, or *almost* nothing—the blue Mont Blanc, she decided, might have been his after all. Before she left, Pars Mansoor came to her cottage to say good-bye. He was taking a later flight that afternoon, returning home to Berkeley. They hugged perfunctorily on the deck, and then he placed something in the palm of her hand.

What is it? she asked.

The stone was purple; she vaguely remembered him toying with it days earlier on the bus.

I've had it since I was boy, he explained. It's from Shiraz.

I see. She smiled and held it out to him.

It's for you, he said.

I can't take this, she protested and tried putting it back in his palm.

He held both hands in the air.

No, no, he insisted. You keep it for a while; then, when you're ready, you can give it back.

I can't, she objected.

He crossed his arms and said: You must.

He stepped toward her. He took the sides of her head in his hands and kissed her forehead and said something in Farsi she couldn't understand—though it didn't seem to require translation.

The last to remain were Claartija deJong and Diana Olmstead. They watched the others depart from the inn, one and then another, all through the windy afternoon, with hugs and waves and leaves swirling on the drive, but no promises of seeing each other again, for what could possibly be the occasion?

After the others had left, Diana Olmstead hobbled down to the sea. There were thirty-eight days left of the *bardo* state. Thirty-eight more days for her on the island. She set herself on the boulder and crossed her good leg and took out her prayer beads. Claartija watched from the top of the steps, then turned back toward the house. Kevin, meanwhile, had climbed upstairs to his bedroom. Douglas was gone to work, and Kevin closed the door behind. It had been a very long few days, and what he needed now, more than anything, was sleep.

III

SEVENTEEN

Bird migration in the north largely ceases sometime in late autumn. The wood warblers are among the first songbirds to go. Their brilliant summer plumage—orange, vermilion, blue—fades as fall approaches. The next to leave are sparrows—Fox and Clay-Colored and Chipping—then the wrens and Catharus thrushes. By November, it's flickers and woodcocks, each exiting at the appropriate time. The last to leave are the kingfishers. They linger as long as possible in the north, wherever the water hasn't frozen. Solitary, unpartnered, they rattle over their small stretches of river or pond or tidal pool. In Germany they're called "icebirds" for the way they retreat southward in front of freezing water. Yet even kingfishers must migrate, however short a distance, when a hard freeze glazes their fishing grounds.

* * *

On Trachis Island that year, a Belted Kingfisher remained the entire winter, a single male *Megaceryle alcyon*. Kevin Gearns noticed it one frigid morning while walking Oscar along the beach. The Trachis Bird Club noted it as well in their annual newsletter, and on their Christmas Bird Count. No one could remember the last time a kingfisher had overwintered on the island.

For Kevin, it was a terribly long winter at Trachis Inn. Diana Olmstead was the last of the family members to depart; she stayed the full forty-nine days as planned, sending the souls of the dead off to their new incarnations. The forty-ninth day happened to coincide with the eve of All Saints' Day. *Coincidence?* Kevin asked.

Diana Olmstead only smiled. She took his hands in both of hers, then climbed into the van back home, rolled the window, and said: Trick or Treat.

By late October, others had begun arriving at Trachis Inn. They were no longer family members but investigators with the Canadian Transportation Safety Board, airline officials, men from the FBI, the RCMP. Rooms were in demand. Everyone wanted to stay on the island; everyone wanted to get close to the site. What could Kevin do? He had to keep the inn open. He couldn't shut it down as they did each fall.

By the end of November he was worn out. It was one thing to care for the families, quite another to host a parade of airplane officials, investigators, pathologists, those who'd come late to the table, whose connection with the crash seemed tenuous at best. They banged cell phones that didn't work. They dragged blackboards into the drawing room, made charts of wiring and voltage buses, left napkins on the table inked with diagrams of the cockpit, then demanded, incredibly, that their pictures be taken beside the bluffs. There were the professional air disaster people who showed up too: journalists, lawyers, conspiracy theorists, those who blamed the Dutch airline—and by association the Dutch themselves. How could anyone blame the Dutch? Kevin wondered. For tulips? Hydroengineering? For Gouda and dikes?

He grew sick of it all. When would it end? When would they stop coming? When could he have his well-earned winter? For he loved the Trachis winters, when all the summer cottages were closed and the island tucked into itself, a closed shell, a clam: the snow squalls in the afternoons, fires in the hearth, and the short, pink twilights with the sun racing into the sea. In winter on Trachis the stars burned brighter than any other time of year. That winter Kevin had planned to purchase a telescope. He'd wanted one since they'd moved to the island, and he'd promised himself for his birthday this year, he'd buy one; Douglas promised too. He'd set it up in the bedroom with a Peterson guide and finally he'd learn the constellations: the Pleiades, Orion, Cygnus, the Bear; hadn't he deserved it? He'd turned fifty-two earlier that summer. And each year seemed like a card in a deck—and *this* one was *definitely* the Joker. But was it too much to ask for a telescope? Was it too much, after fifty-two years on earth—fifty-two years he hadn't thought he'd survive—to be able to look up at night and name another object besides the moon?

Not this year. Douglas had typically forgotten. And who could think of the stars or birthdays or anything else aside from the guests, with their speculations and theories, their book binders, and outside the constant drone of recovery ships still plying the waters off the coast.

Each time Kevin drove past Caginish Point that November he saw cars from out of province: tour buses, engines chugging in the cold, knots of people hunched into the icy winds. Voyeurs. Some with camcorders. All with cameras. He wanted to chase them away. Why did they need to come? What use was their presence, rubbernecking, trampling down the teaberry and pitcher plants? Why did they need to travel so far just to get within arm's reach of death? To inhale it, to photograph it. To say they were there; they'd seen the spot. Did it make them somehow stronger to rub elbows with the dead? Did they say: *This could have been me?* Wild strawberries bloomed there each June, and every year Kevin had picked them. They were small, tart, tastier than the cultivated kind. But not next year; he wouldn't pick strawberries at Caginish ever again.

One night an American couple arrived who claimed they'd lost their son on the flight. After registering, they went down to the beach with metal detectors. Kevin had a nagging feeling. Who would do such a thing? Douglas checked them out at the naval yard; he was working there full-time, helping with the sorting. No, they'd never heard of the couple; they weren't on any of the family lists. Bunty Phillips ended up escorting them off the island and telling them never to return.

The tinfoil set, Douglas chimed.

Tinfoil?

He'd learned the word from a veteran crash investigator. They showed up at every air disaster.

But *tinfoil?* Kevin asked.

They wear tinfoil under their hats, Douglas explained—as if it was the most obvious thing in the world. It keeps aliens from reading their minds.

* * *

Somewhere in a laboratory in Ottawa that fall, men in lab coats burned bits of electrical wire, plunged them into salt water, placed them against litmus paper and compared the colors with those of the burnt wires found on the plane. Another man studied the filaments of lightbulbs, the manner in which they twisted when burned. Another freeze-dried documents found floating on the water: napkins, newspapers, business reports, a page of musical notation (*The Metamorphoses* by Richard Strauss). Later, they'd all be examined for a message, a mark, a clue, some indication those onboard had known what was going on. Slowly, meticulously, over months, the plane itself was being hung back together, each piece—some no larger than a postage stamp—stuck onto a life-size skeleton the exact shape of the plane. A giant jigsaw puzzle, a shattered cup, two hundred and fifty tons heavy.

None of this mattered to Kevin Gearns. It wouldn't change a thing. Yet each night, when he came home from the naval yard, Douglas rattled on about ailerons and Kapton cable and the in-flight entertainment system and emergency cockpit procedures, until Kevin finally had to tell him to stop. He didn't want to hear it anymore.

Why all this fuss for people who'd died so publicly—so spectacularly—in a flash, when there was nothing for the thousands who'd died agonizingly slow, alone, shunned inside their rooms? Was this what was eating away at Kevin for weeks? All the friends in New York City he'd watched die *and no one cared*?

Yet Douglas, who was too young to have experienced those years in New York, needed to talk. Ever since that night at Government Dock, working side by side with the search and rescue volunteers, he'd been galvanized. What happened the weeks following at the naval yard Douglas couldn't quite put into words; but he'd worked with people from all over the provinces who felt personally responsible for solving the puzzle of the crash. It had become something of an obsession for them, and Douglas, sensing their focus, their fervor, found it intoxicating too. With each recovery of an engine part, a wing flap, an electrical panel, they felt closer to an answer. Some nights after work, Douglas shared a beer with two young naval officers and some of the other workers. And after the excitement of the sorting facility and the camaraderie of the bar, Douglas found himself often reluctant to return home. Kevin could be such an old fart sometimes—he simply refused even to *discuss* the crash. He cared only about the upkeep of the inn, and complained about all the things Douglas wasn't helping with. For years, they'd been drifting apart, two pieces of plankton floating farther and farther away. But now the gulf between them grew even greater. It wasn't just the dozen years between them. It seemed to Douglas at times that Kevin cared more for his guests than he did for Douglas himself. And while Kevin complained about Douglas's lack of help, wasn't it that Kevin wouldn't *let* him do anything? Wasn't he just such a fucking control freak?

The darkest days of winter arrived. The wind batted and tore at the house. The Fallons, the neighbors with the summer cottage, pestered Kevin again with calls from Montreal. Would he *please* check their cottage, the hot water heater, the fridge? Could he get someone to drain the pipes?

By December, he felt something stirring inside. Breaking, snapping, coring itself out. He felt like a piece of wood, whittled down—thin, sharp, irritable. He longed for the silent Bulgarian, the Dutch girl, for Pars Mansoor and Ana Gathreaux. Those first days after the crash seemed almost innocent now, if that could possibly be said. For there had been such an outpouring from every person on the island, from the fishermen, the islanders, everyone offering rooms, cars, homes, the signs on the lawns expressing their solidarity. Kevin had felt it too, an orgy of public grief, of love.

It was all gone now, evaporated, a summer's dew. Even the island fishermen, who'd gone out that first night in the fog and risked their lives among the sharp fragments of the plane— even they grew embittered; for since the crash they couldn't launch their boats, and the waters remained off limits. They'd hosted families from New York City, from Amsterdam, but what had *they* gotten in return? When could they fish again? When could they have their island back?

Some afternoons when the main house was full, Kevin escaped to the frozen garden. He sat on the bench in the cold among the bolted lettuces, the split cabbage, the dead cucumber vines. Tomatoes hung frozen on their stalks. Pumpkins sagged and rotted in the center. A fringe of isinglass glistened on the walkway. When would all of this stop? he wondered. When would life return as before? He kept thinking of the Auden poem about the Brueghel painting, the boy dropping into the sea. It was Icarus, he remembered now, falling into the water (he finally found the book). If only he could be like the plowman or the ship, ignoring the splash. *It was not an important failure; the sun shone as it had to on the white legs disappearing into the green.* That was how it went . . . *and the expensive delicate ship. . . sailed calmly on.*

EIGHTEEN

Ana Gathreaux's first days back on Ninth Street passed like a silent film: the sun rose and fell, traffic inched up the avenue—yet nothing seemed to make any noise. The afternoons were chilled, bright, the mornings unassailably blue. There was so much for her to do: agree to some kind of memorial, a service, a funeral; people kept asking, volunteering to arrange one—but surely she couldn't have a memorial if Russell hadn't yet been found. There was Russell's mother to visit in England; she called every other day and left long, woeful messages on Ana's machine—as if *she* were the one most bereft. There was the lab to contend with. Russell's office at the museum. Friends came to the loft and left food. Cakes. Lasagna. Cookies. After they went, Ana threw their baking in the trash, or put it on the roof for the pigeons. She couldn't possibly be expected to eat cake.

In her lab, the Savannah Sparrows fluttered in their cages,

twitched their wings when they saw her, begged the way they would as chicks when a parent approached. Her lab assistant looked on, delighted, clasping hands.

They missed you! Connie exclaimed, but Ana turned away.
Please, she said, I can't . . .

She locked herself in the bathroom and wept.

She avoided the loft. The place seemed sentient, full of Russell's presence, his pocket change, his pants, a used tissue beneath the bed (she realized now *that too* would've worked for DNA). She was afraid to touch anything, the toaster, the computer—even the tissue. Yvonne offered to come over and scour the place. The sooner you make it yours, she advised, the better. But how could Ana touch anything or remove his things—his shoes, his shirts, his papers—before she had a body, before it was official, before the piece of paper arrived that said he was no longer? *Habeas corpus.* "You should have the body." Shouldn't *she* have the body? How did one say that in Latin? Surely Russell would have known.

It was somehow easier to visit the loft in the evenings, around dusk or later, when the lights were out and the radiators hissed and she'd pick through the pile of condolences gingerly, afraid to handle too many at a time. They came from around the world: from friends, colleagues, people she'd never even heard of. Someone in Thailand. Public school friends from England (how they'd gotten his address, she didn't know). The clock in the loft was off by an hour; no one had turned it back that fall. The plants lay dead in the kitchen window and on the roof. Ana put the mail aside and sat on the bed in the twilight, the blue counterpane, the one they'd brought back from England, still on the mattress. She'd close her eyes and wait for the sound of his footfalls, his key in the door, the click of the lock, thinking, It could happen; he could come home; she could have the body. Would he come? Did he know she was waiting? A girl shouted *"chinga!"* in the street. A grate slid shut for the night. When she opened her eyes, the headlights were backed up to Brooklyn on the Williamsburg Bridge. Planes lowered over rooftops across the river. One every few minutes blinking into LaGuardia, so many planes each hour, each day. What were the odds that one wouldn't return from the sky?

At her lab, there was the unavoidable parade of colleagues. They stopped her in the hall, knocked meekly on her door, offered her what words they could (inadequate, fumbling) or slipped small notes in her box (kind, a bit cowardly). She had to endure all that. A second death—of words.

Yvonne forced her outside for lunch one afternoon. They sat at Veselka in the chill sunlight of Second Avenue, Ana crouched behind a pair of sunglasses. She ought to see someone, Yvonne said. She ought to get drugs. Counseling. She didn't have to walk around like that (but what if she *wanted* to walk around like that? What if she *wanted* to feel sorry for herself?). Her brother, Peter, kept calling from Long Island, inviting her out. He even drove into the city once—which made Ana feel only worse, the two of them together in his car, with nothing at all to say. All everyone wanted to hear from her was that *she was okay.* She was *coping.* She wouldn't slit her wrists, stick her head in the oven, leap into the East River. But she couldn't tell them that. And why should she? Why this insistence on being *fine,* on staying alive, her heart continuing its usual tidy beat?

* * *

The only time she felt slightly better, the only time when she thought, Perhaps life will go on, in a different way now— how she didn't know—was when, at night, she phoned Pars Mansoor. He'd written his number on a five-dollar Canadian bill before he left Trachis Island; and she kept it now on her desk in the lab along with the purple stone. Talking to Pars, more than to anyone else, gave her a glimpse of hope, a crack in the clouds. It was different from talking to Yvonne or Peter, or any of her colleagues or friends; yes, they were sympathetic, shocked, moved, terribly grieved themselves; but Pars had *been there* on the island all those days, and he understood something else. What had he told her once, that Jews had the corner on guilt, Catholics sin, but Persians were the connoisseurs of grief? That in Iran there was an expression: *Gosseh Khordan,* to "eat sorrow." Hadn't they both eaten the same raw sorrow?

Sometimes when she talked to Pars, minutes passed on the phone and neither of them said anything, but the silences were not unbearable. They were empty vessels, a cup, a bucket that hung, and didn't need to be filled right away, or ever. She pictured him across the continent in Berkeley, on the other end of the line, the receiver by his ear, a scoop to gather grains of silence. One night, late in her office, she heard twinkling on the other end of the phone.

It must be sunset there, she remarked.

How do you know? he asked.

I can hear it.

She had her feet up on the desk. It was ten at night in New York City.

Hold on, he said.

She heard him move a chair or a desk. Then she heard a very

distinct gnashing sound. He was holding the receiver out the window. A second later he returned to the phone.

What do you hear?

Swifts, she said. They're probably high over the building. They're crepuscular.

Good word, he said. What does it mean?

They come out at twilight, she explained. They feed at that time.

May I use it?

The swifts?

No, the word.

Sure. She laughed. It's all yours.

They both fell silent. She was thinking: Crepuscular. It sounded like "corpuscle" and "muscular," only different from both. She heard him going back inside, the window closing.

Lawyers had called him, he said. They were starting a suit against the airline and they needed information. And there was another thing: they'd positively identified Lailah. He'd gotten the call that morning.

God, she whispered.

Yes.

He knew better than to ask about Russell. If they'd called her with anything, she'd have told him. He said he was thinking of returning to Iran to see his sister. They talked for a while longer, but Ana felt the wind go out of her sails. She was relieved for Pars and his family, yet she couldn't help but think: Why not Russell? Why hadn't he been identified?

Pars exhaled on the other end of the line. She could no longer hear the sound of the swifts.

Is it all right, he asked, that I called?

Yes, she said and wanted to tell him, he was one of the few

things she looked forward to, his slightly lilting voice, a kind of ladder she could climb. But she didn't say any of that. Instead she said she'd call the next night, or the night after.

November arrived. The days were empty amphitheaters, each filled with light, then dark, then light. She lit a Kaddish candle a Jewish friend had given her with Hebrew lettering on the glass. The lawyers called her too. She made lists of famous people who had died in plane crashes (*Buddy Holly, Will Rogers, Roberto Clemente*). She asked everyone she knew. Did they form a confederacy of their own, those who'd dropped from the sky? (*Patsy Cline, Glenn Miller, Guido Cantelli.*) Those who sublimated from air to air, or into water first? (*Ritchie Valens, Amelia Earhart, Dag Hammarskjöld.*) Someone told her—stupidly, as if it would help—that diving into water was a metaphor the ancients used for a good death: the waters of oblivion. The sarcophagus from Paestum (*Icarus,* someone said, *the first known victim of flight*).

The holidays grew near. Lawyers left messages, sent forms in the mail. She was supposed to make copies of Russell's tax returns. They wanted to know his net worth. The calculus bewildered her. The value based on his potential future earnings, on 1040 forms. A man apparently was worth more than a woman. A white more than a black; a young man more than an old. (An American more than just about anyone else.) But how much was a body, any body, really worth? How much for the nitrogen, carbon, oxygen, the hair, the bone? Thirty-nine cents, she recalled from high school biology. Thirty-nine cents; perhaps more for living blood. But she had no body, not even a bone. Each time the phone rang she held her breath. She let the forms pile up. What could she possibly tell the lawyers of her husband's potential worth?

* * *

One afternoon in December, Pars called her in the lab.

Where are you? she asked.

The Strand, he said.

The beach?

No. Broadway and Twelfth.

It took a moment to register. There were horns honking on the other end of the line.

You're in *Manhattan*?

I'm in Manhattan.

Her heart leapt. For a moment she felt light-headed, confused, terribly distraught.

Don't move, she said. I'll be right up there.

Before she hung up he told her: he'd be in poetry.

She was somehow not surprised—nothing surprised her lately. She pulled on her coat, her beret. Sprayed deodorant beneath her sweater to cover her lack of showering. She was afraid to see Pars. Afraid *not* to see him. Outside, the skies were lead; a damp wind ripped up the avenues. She stopped at a shop window on the corner of Eleventh and checked her teeth in the glass. How gaunt she looked. How haggard. She fixed her beret on her head. For some inane reason she felt a twinge of infidelity. She took a tube of lipstick from her bag, but thought better of it and tossed it back inside.

At the bookstore, Pars was up a ladder, coat folded over one arm.

Parviz? she said.

He almost stumbled off the ladder. His face erupted into a

smile, then he colored and climbed down and they half hugged, with his coat between them.

What a surprise, she said. What are you *doing* here?

He showed her the book in his hand.

I was looking for Hafiz.

I mean *here*—she stamped a foot—*New York*.

Well—he shrugged, I'll tell you . . . But he didn't finish his sentence. He was looking at her instead.

How are you?

How do you think I am?

They stood, face-to-face a moment. Ana grew suddenly self-conscious. After all the phone calls, he'd become just a voice, a message on her machine; and seeing him now in the flesh, she felt slightly deflated. What did he want from her? What did *she* want? He was still staring at her. She grew hot in her sweater. Pars shifted his coat to his opposite arm. They both looked at the floor.

Come, he said, I'll pay for this and we'll go.

She wiped perspiration from her forehead, and they made their way to the front of the store. Pars said he'd finally found Hafiz, but he was in the wrong section.

Poor Hafiz. He shook his head. He wasn't in poetry at all. They put him in New Age, can you believe that? He's more than two hundred years older than Mr. Shakespeare, yet they call him "New."

He got on line at the cashier while she waited by the door.

Outside, it was lunch hour. Pars shouldered a small black bag. The wind spiraled scraps of newsprint in the air. In Union

Square, the Salvation Army was already ringing bells. Usually that time of year, Ana and Russell flew to his mother's in East Anglia for a week. Not this year. There wasn't any *usual* this year.

Pars had arrived just that morning on a red-eye. He hadn't eaten since the night before, and Ana suggested they get some lunch. She knew a place in the Twenties, an Indian restaurant. Pars said fine.

They walked up Broadway. Pars had never been in Manhattan before and he kept turning around, pirouetting at buildings, the sidewalks, the people.

So, Ana said, you came all this way for lunch?

No. He shook his head. His sister and her husband were flying over from Iran. He was going to meet them in Montreal in a few days. Since he was flying east, he decided . . .

He made a vague gesture with one hand, then pushed the glasses up the bridge of his nose.

To what? Ana asked.

To check on you, he said.

He stopped in his path and stared across the street at the Flatiron Building.

What an amazing building, he said. Does it have a name?

Yes, she said, it does, and she told him.

The restaurant was off Fifth. It was one of Russell's favorites, a cafeteria with the best *idlis* in New York. Ana often met him there after work.

Inside, the lunch crowd was thinning. The windows steamed. Pars ordered a chicken *saag,* Ana a vegetarian plate. When she reached the checkout, Ana realized her mistake. The friendly woman with the bindi and the glass bangles was working the register.

How is the husband? she asked.

Ana fished a bill from her wallet.

Fine, she muttered.

I have not seen him in some time. Tell him we are missing him.

Ana smiled tensely and took her change. The woman nodded thanks for the tip.

At the table, Pars was waiting. Ana set her tray down and looked at the plate of steaming dal. She'd pretty much lost her appetite.

Later, she brought Pars back to her loft. She hadn't been there in two days. It was odd having Pars there; he seemed to provide some kind of protection, a force field. He paced the wooden floors, picked books off the shelf. Ana boiled water for tea. On the bookshelf were bound issues of *The Auk*. Pyle's *Identification Guide to North American Passerines*. *The Bird Collectors* by Barbara and Richard Mearns. Bub's *Bird Trapping and Banding*. Pars pulled out a copy of *Cladistics*.

He's got an article in that one. Ana pointed with the teapot.

Russell does, she added.

Really, Pars said.

She brought the tea to the kitchen table. Pars sat with the journal. The pot steamed in the cold sunlight. There were shoes in the corner. Weejuns. Size eight. Out the window the traffic on the bridge was an alloy of fluid steel.

Where are you staying? Ana asked.

A Holiday Inn.

I didn't even know there was one.

I think it's on Lafayette, he said.

She set two brown cups with saucers on the table and began pouring milk into each, then stopped herself.

Oh crap. I forgot. No milk.

It doesn't matter, he said.

She took the cup and dumped it in the sink, came back with a small glass and sugar bowl.

You remember?

Yes, she said. Russell was very particular about his tea. Two bags of Typhoo, three minutes in the pot. Milk first. Tea on top. I remember.

She poured the tea into his glass, and then filled her own cup.

Pars spooned sugar, two, three, then four teaspoons into the glass.

He looked up at her guiltily while stirring.

It's a family habit, he confessed.

He removed the Strand bag from his coat pocket and pushed it across the wooden table.

This is for you, he said.

She put her cup down.

Please, not another gift.

Okay. Consider it a loan.

She took the book from the bag—*Selected Poems of Hafiz*—and opened the cover tentatively.

In Iran, Pars explained, there's a tradition of using Hafiz for telling fortunes. A bit like the *I Ching.* Except with Hafiz, he said, you open to any page and it gives you the fortune.

Convenient, Ana said.

Hafiz was a chemist, Pars continued. But also one of the great Persian poets. In the gardens around his tomb in Shiraz, he told her, there used to be an old man who carried an enormous diwan of his poems. The old man had a piece of cardboard with hundreds of numbers painted on it, and a cockatiel that always perched on his shoulder. You paid him a coin and he let the bird land on a number on the cardboard—and that was the number of your poem. He'd open the great book and read it to you, and there was your fortune. In our house, Pars said, we simply flipped the book and read whatever page we'd opened to.

Interesting, Ana said.

She studied the book. Pars sipped from his glass.

Do I have to do it now? she asked.

No. Pars shook his head. You don't have to do it all. It's the poems. They're what's important.

She set the book aside and thanked him and picked up her tea. Pars blew on his glass. They sat together in silence, the tea sending steam into the afternoon, one helix from his glass, another from her cup. Even though the sun was still out, a few snow flurries began drifting across the roof.

Pars stayed for three days. He slept on a spare futon the first night. The second night, they slept in the same bed, fully clothed, as they had on the island. She took him on the subway, showed him the Empire State Building, the Museum of Modern Art. He wanted to see Coney Island because of the Ferlinghetti poem; and they rode out on the F train and walked through the shuttered park as rain fell on the boardwalk and over the Cyclone and out at sea. Why, she wondered aloud, were they always ending up at the ocean?

Afterward, on the ride back, the streets fled past: Avenue X and Y, the entire alphabet slick with rain. She fell asleep against

his shoulder, as she had the first afternoon on the bus on Trachis Island; yet this time it was different, though she couldn't
say how.

She woke once underground, Pars tapping her shoulder.

Do we need to get off sometime soon? he inquired.

No, she said. They were only at Jay Street–Borough Hall.
She closed her eyes again. They had four more stops to go.

For three days, she didn't go back to her lab. She returned no
one's calls. She felt like a fugitive inside her own loft. It was
good to have a body in her bed. Someone she barely knew.
Someone who understood. Someone, she kept thinking, whom
Russell would have liked. Would he care? Did it matter? Wasn't
it only survival, one body with another? A fugue, that was the
word Mrs. McIntyre used for Mrs. Liang. A fugue was a musical piece in polyphonic form, where a theme was introduced
by one, harmonized by another and then another, contrapun-
tally, and reintroduced throughout. Yet it was also the name for
a momentary flight from reality, an amnesia, brought on by
monumental stress. That was what had happened, they said,
to Mrs. Liang. Why she'd ended up incoherent in the lighthouse on Trachis Island. But wasn't that too what was happen-
ing now to Ana? A fugue. An escape. A flight from reality? In
these last few days at least. Wasn't she too trying simply to
escape?

On the day Pars left, he stood with his bag by the door and
they kissed, and it was something slightly more than just a
good-bye kiss—but not *much* more. She asked him to call as
soon as he returned home. He squeezed her hand in parting.
He smelled a bit like pine needles.

* * *

Was it good to see him? Yes. No. She wasn't sure. But after he left, she closed the loft door behind him and stood with her back to it and wept; she felt relieved and saddened and confused all at once, but mostly relief, that he was gone. The loft was empty again. It belonged to her and Russell, as it should. Outside, on the roof, the dead miscanthus shivered in the wind. The Japanese maple. She went to the kitchen table. The Hafiz was still there, where they'd left it days ago in its Strand bag. She remembered what he'd said about the cockatiel, the augur, and she fanned the pages bravely, tearily, stopped at random, then opened the spine and read:

> *This Sky where we live*
> *Is no place to lose your wings.*
> *So love, love,*
> *Love*

NINETEEN

On Trachis Island the days grew long. The nights brought freezing rain, then snow, then sleet. The recovery ships pulled anchor and steamed away, and once again the sea offshore was left in silence. Kittiwakes keened. The bays froze solid. Murres bobbed and dove into the icy foam.

At night a brace of stars hung over Trachis Inn; and what was Kevin Gearns to do at last but close the place? He couldn't take it anymore, the endless guests—airline insurers, friends of the departed, Boeing executives. The false thaw passed, the first of February came. And finally, he did what he'd been threatening for months: He said no. He wouldn't have any more guests. He was closing the doors, locking out the world, even though they called and faxed and e-mailed. If Douglas was around, he might have changed his mind, but by February he was gone for good. Not only during the days but during the nights as well. He'd gotten a job on the mainland, in another hangar where they sorted bits of the broken fuselage; his dream job (for he always did like puzzles). How he'd gotten the job, Kevin didn't know—and Douglas didn't offer—yet for weeks he'd moved about the house secretive and vague about his comings and goings. For weeks he'd spent hours online at night, in the office, and when Kevin approached, he'd sheepishly change the screen. Kevin suspected an affair; it wouldn't be the first time—and probably not the last. But what was Kevin to do, make a scene, protest, demand answers? He was too weary for all that.

Go! Kevin shouted, when Douglas told him about the job. And he surprised himself by the passion in his voice; for he felt no passion, only exhaustion. With the confusion and trauma of the last few months, he was too tired to fight, to make demands. He'd let Douglas go (perhaps he'd even pushed him). In truth Kevin was a bit relieved to have him out of the house.

Finally, Kevin put the sign on the Peninsular Road "Closed for the Season" and ran the chain across the drive. The first night he built a blazing fire in the hearth. He poured himself a scotch and sat alone in the drawing room with the dog curled beside him on the couch; and he let loose what he'd been holding inside him for months, ever since the crash: a howl, a threnody. Were any of his tears for Douglas? Yes. Perhaps some. They'd grown so distant; some nights they slept in separate rooms. But it was more than Douglas he mourned. It was all these long months of running the inn without a break, without time to take stock of what had become of their lives.

* * *

So the house curled in on itself, a cowrie closed off to all others. The rooms unpeopled, the library, the drawing room, every corner and hallway and stair. At night Kevin haunted the empty rooms. He pulled Oscar into bed with him and slept beside the dog despite the sand, despite his breath, despite whatever he'd rolled in the day before. For what other comfort was there on a winter night alone in a big house by the sea? The moon stared in through every window, accompanied him into each room; entered casements and double panes, so that in each quarter, there it was painting a glass here, a vase there, a picture frame, a mirror. Any shiny surface welcomed it: the toaster, the pier glass in the hall. And who knew, on a winter night like this, beneath the waves, beneath the moon, the ocean continued its business under layers of foam and ice, the dark machinery churning with one eye on the planets, the other on the land; and in the littoral zones, directly in the bay, hadn't he seen in summer days, the clear aquarium beneath the waves, a brilliant aqueous garden of seaweed and bladder wrack, and strands of orange hairs? The white hydrangea-leafed water plant that looked like bridal veils (like bridesmaids standing under the sea), the green velvet tubes called "dead man's fingers"? Who knew on a slender night in February that life continued under there, silent and unseen by human eyes?

The nights grew moderate. March arrived. Some days the earth breathed again, a sigh of oniongrass. The days turned almost languid. Crocuses erupted on the lawn. The house was Kevin's alone, a kingdom, a cave. He retreated to the library and took out his old books, those he hadn't opened since graduate school—so long ago! And at night, with the pages of his unfinished dissertation spread before him (untethered now from their rubber bands, their paper clips), he sat beside the fire

with his old friends: Ovid, Pythagoras, Heraclitus. He reread
Ovid's *Teachings of Pythagoras*; it had been the basis of his dissertation. But what was Kevin on to back then, something he'd
since forgotten and now—twenty years later, on these equi-
noctial nights—he tried to make sense of again? Pythagoras's
idea of metempsychosis? Heraclitus's belief in universal flux,
in the flame? Kevin had tried—and failed—to connect both
Heraclitus and Pythagoras with Lao Tsu and Buddha Sakya-
muni. The Western philosophers with the Eastern. They'd all
been alive at roughly the same time—500 B.C.—and surely
they had all drunk from the same source. Kevin's Ph.D. adviser
said that his dissertation draft was "bold" but "scattered" and
"unfocused"; he needed to make it more cogent. And where
did Ovid fit into all this anyhow? Where did *reincarnation*?
Kevin was so young at the time, so insensible to half of it. And
just about the same time, all his friends in New York began
falling ill. So he'd put the dissertation aside and taken care of
one and then another friend; and the plague years came and
passed and the dissertation remained untouched—still in its
cardboard box.

Now, those spring nights on Trachis, he pored over the
pages once more. He may have been too young to comprehend
it all back then—for death hadn't surrounded him yet. But
now the Heraclitean flame made stunning sense to him. For
wasn't each person he ever knew, living or dead, a candle that
had flickered for a few years and then went out—his mother
and father and all his friends who'd passed, his young nephews
so recently kindled, who would extinguish just as well. "All
things change to fire, and fire exhausted, falls back into
things." Hadn't all of the dead in his life simply "fallen back
into things"?

Kevin slept late in the mornings. At night, in the drawing room, the sound of the surf was a sentence that kept starting over and over but never finished. The ocean hurled entreaties at the land. What was it trying to say? What was the line that needed completion?

In April the spring tide was enormous. Monumental on the full-moon night. The tide erased the beach, disfigured the dunes, overran the sand with dulse and devil's apron; and the half shells of scallops were castanets torn in two.

On the hillsides, forsythia flamed and the wind ran brilliant over darkened fields. The garden lay in ruins. Could Kevin possibly plant anew? Start another garden? It all seemed a dream, the last seven months. The plane, the guests. The Bulgarian. Diana Olmstead, the Dutch girl.

Go! he'd shouted and was surprised afterward by his reserve of passion, the trembling in his voice, but also: *that Douglas actually went*. Kevin never expected that.

One night late in April, Kevin picked up the phone. He'd been sleeping in front of the fire when it rang, his copy of Heraclitus's *Fragments* opened on the coffee table, an empty glass of scotch. There was static on the line. He couldn't quite hear the voice but knew: It was Douglas. He was calling from a pay phone in a bar in Halifax.

It's me, Douglas said uncertainly, and Kevin said he knew. And after a pause that seemed to last forever, Douglas finally asked: What went wrong? Why didn't we ever talk?

Kevin had no answer. He was barely awake. He could hear the sound of video games in the background. Finally he said: I don't know, Doug. I don't know why we never did.

Let's, Douglas offered.

He sounded like he'd been drinking, but Kevin didn't care.

Okay, he said cautiously.

And so they agreed that night on the phone. Douglas would drive down the next morning. He'd catch the noon or the one o'clock ferry. They'd sit in the kitchen or outside on the stone terrace and finally, after all this time, they would talk.

TWENTY

The last Friday in May that spring, Laura Fallon and her two daughters caught the early ferry to Trachis Island. The morning was brisk. Coral clouds hovered overhead. The ocean breathed ice, but the sun was warm on the boat.

The girls—Isabel and Olivia—raced along the upper deck, past red-and-white painted rowboats. Excited, sprinting, the sea wind in their hair, they'd been stuck in the city all spring and winter. For eight months they'd begged to go out to the island; they'd pleaded and whined, but their father wouldn't allow them. It wasn't a good time to visit Trachis, he said. Not with the recovery ships offshore and the island overrun with rescue teams and searchers, and with what the girls were likely to see by their beach house: bits of plane carted onshore. Men scouring the strand. God knows what drifting in on the tide. If they saw any of that, they'd never step foot again on a plane—let alone in the ocean. It was best to wait until the island sorted itself out. They'd have to stay in their town house in Montreal until then.

Just after the crash, Mark Fallon had called Kevin Gearns from Montreal. Kevin lived just up the road on Trachis. He asked if Kevin would walk over and check on the place, throw away the food in the fridge (and take whatever he wanted). And did he know someone who could drain the pipes, turn off the hot water heater, the fridge, and board the windows for winter? Kevin suggested Sheila Quinn's brother Rupert (he certainly could use the money). Mark Fallon took the number and thanked him. Kevin said he'd give Rupert the key.

That was last September, and though Mark had asked Rupert Quinn to put a bill in the mail, no bill had arrived all winter; and Mark and Laura worried if Kevin had even given him the key, if the windows had been boarded and the gas turned off, the pipes drained. And what of the lawn and the garden and the beach? Was the little blue rowboat still left outside? Had Rupert Quinn seen to that too?

On any normal year, the Fallons would have gone to Trachis for the Christmas holiday (cold walks on the beach, fires in the Waterford stove). But not this year. The island was still in turmoil. They stayed in Montreal instead, skied the Laurentians. Yet with the first hint of warm weather, the girls began anew: *When will we go to the island? When can we get to the beach?* Soon, soon, said Mark Fallon, but he had his TV show to attend to, scripts to keep up with, new ones to write. Couldn't they go for just a few days? Laura pleaded.

Finally, Laura decided: She'd go on her own with the girls. She'd never done the twelve-hour drive without her husband, but the girls were old enough now; Olivia could take care of

Isabel. They'd spend a night at a motel along the way. Mark could stay in town with his scripts. It was already May besides. Surely the island was safe to return to. God knew Laura could use a break as well. From Mark. From Montreal. From the same six rooms.

Olivia stood beside the wooden rail, her braid between her teeth (a habit she'd just started). Isabel held a potato chip in the air to feed the jockeying gulls. Buoys moaned in the bay. Laura put an arm around both girls.

Smell that air, she said and inhaled deeply the familiar salt air, the diesel, the North Atlantic breeze.

Farther out, the girls scanned the horizon, looking for the Trachis Lighthouse. Each time they arrived, they had a contest as to who could see the lighthouse first (inevitably it ended up with Isabel in tears). Mark had started the game once on a rough ferry ride when the girls were very young, to keep them from getting sick: Looking at the horizon was the best thing for *mal de mer.* But since then spotting the lighthouse first had turned into a competition. It didn't help that Mark invented tales about the lighthouse: bedtime stories he told about the family who lived in the lighthouse, the daughter of the lighthouse keeper, the sailor she'd rescued at sea, who'd become half man, half fish: a merman.

When he first told the story, Olivia protested.

Daddy, she said. There are no mermaids, and certainly no mer*mans.*

Quite the contrary, Mark said and told them about the Danish Havmand, the German Nix, and the Chinese Hai Ho Shang—all manfish (the last a Buddhist monk!). He'd just been researching a screenplay, and the names were fresh in mind.

Olivia was about to argue when her father put a finger to his lips and winked to seal the conspiracy between them—at the expense of Isabel (who was not yet four at the time and who lay rapt in the bottom bunk).

Olivia was smiling now.

Tell us about the merman, Olivia said, picking up the thread. And he did.

Sometimes the story changed. Sometimes the shipwrecked sailor was a real person, other times he became a selkie or a merman or a succubus. But the lighthouse keeper's daughter was always the same, always steadfast and brave, always risking her life to save drowned sailors. Sometimes she became an Olympic swimmer. Other times she stayed at the lighthouse, rescuing people or dolphins or whales (Mark *was* a screenwriter after all). Each night in August, he told them the stories before bed, as the green arm of the lighthouse rounded into their room and Olivia lay on the top bunk and Isabel on the bottom. What made the stories even more mysterious was that some nights they could see the lighthouse and others, because of the fog, it disappeared entirely.

I saw it! I saw it! Isabel screeched. It was *me,* Mommy, I saw it first!

She was pointing into the wind. Trachis Light, a small speck, a flash of a coin on the horizon.

Olivia shrugged.

Big deal, she muttered.

She was just learning the uses of indifference; and the result was immediate. Isabel's face deflated. It was wonderful for Olivia to see. Isabel didn't understand: Why wouldn't Olivia *at least argue?* If only their father was there, *he'd* care. Isabel stalked off toward the plastic seats, mumbling to herself that she'd seen it first.

Later, downstairs in the hold, they sat in the Volvo, watching the approaching pilings through the front of the ferry. The boat weaved. Ropes tightened. Doors slid back. The girls pressed forward in their seats (to see it again, the harbor, the boats, the gulls!). Engines started. Cars began moving. Seat belts! Laura screamed. We can't go *anywhere* until you're in your seat! But Isabel refused to get into the child's seat, and Olivia was chewing again on her braid.

On the island the leaves were just sprouting from trees, tiny lime green flags, so far behind Montreal, where summer had already begun in earnest. The cold hung over the island like an ice cube. There were military trucks parked along the roadsides. Mark had warned Laura: Things might be different. Laura was keyed up as it was; she'd never opened the house for the season alone. The hot water heater gave her the most anxiety; Mark had always done it (the gas frightened her). And she didn't want to bother Rupert Quinn with a call (*why* had he not sent a bill?). The islanders could be so contrary, so proud. She'd probably have to beg Kevin Gearns to come over and help.

Outside the house the purple tulips were blooming. The shutters all in place. So Rupert *had* been there after all. The girls bolted from the car. Laura unlocked the door, took boards off their hinges, opened the windows. She ordered the girls outside. Mice had gotten into the silverware, the soap dish (a cake of Ivory half consumed, a mound of black turds in its stead). There were nests of insulation in the drawers. The house needed a thorough scrubbing, but the girls kept getting in the way.

Off with you, she commanded. Olivia, you look after Isabel, okay?

Olivia nodded her head.

Come, Izzie, she said, let's go to the beach.

First your coats.

But, Mommy!

No buts.

Finally, she watched them go, down through the neighbor's yard, bundled in jackets, even though it was almost June. Olivia led the way.

The morning stirred. Tree Swallows hovered and chirped overhead. Isabel lagged behind, swinging an orange bucket, a stick in one hand; she poked at everything.

Izzie, come on!

But what about the merman? she asked. Was he here?

Where?

In the house, during the winter?

I *doubt* it, Olivia said.

Will we see him on the beach?

Shut up, Izzie.

The ocean was emerald, opalescent by the shore. The bluffs a rich cinnamon red. Olivia scrabbled down to the strand, Isabel followed. Olivia warned her to take it slow. Isabel picked up a mussel shell and deposited it in her bucket. Olivia found the dried carapace of a horseshoe crab and picked it up by its tail.

Izzie, look.

Is it a helmet?

It's the merman's hat.

She held it by the rim above her head.

They wandered farther, past the estuary, among yards of green, translucent seaweed and squiggly tubes that squished beneath their sneakers.

Look, Isabel said.

She picked a large piece of something from the surf; it looked like coral, or like the bone of a small elephant ear or wings, with roundish ends and two hooped handles on the bottom. Was it a sea creature that had washed ashore? A crown? Isabel held it with both hands to her face. Upside down it made a perfect mask; she peered through the two arched sockets in the bottom.

Look, 'Livia, it's the merman's mask!

She stuck it in front of her head, dripping, antlered, and swung from side to side, holding the bone to her face.

Olivia wasn't moving anymore. She stood completely still, the horseshoe crab at her side.

Izzie, I think you should put that down.

Her voice was unusually quiet.

Isabel whirled around with the mask; a little cold seawater dripped on her cheek.

Olivia shouted: Isabel, *put it down!*

Isabel lowered the bone to her side.

What, I found it!

I know, Izzie, it's important, come on.

She turned back toward the house, but Isabel wouldn't follow. Olivia trudged toward her and yanked her hand.

Come on!

Isabel gripped the bone; she wasn't going to give it up that easily. She was sure this was one of her sister's ploys.

* * *

Back up the bluff, Laura had just scrubbed out the sink when she saw the girls through the kitchen window coming over the bluff, one marching after the other, the sun in their hair— Isabel's gold, Olivia's chestnut—Isabel swinging the orange bucket. Oh no, Laura thought, back so soon; they'd fought already, but so quickly? She wiped her forehead with an elbow. She was wearing rubber gloves. There was something about the way they walked, Olivia with her face set, that didn't look right.

Outside, on the lawn, Laura Fallon recognized the bone immediately. It was so obviously a human pelvis, leached of color, ash white, that she jerked a hand involuntarily to her mouth.

Isabel! she screamed. Drop that thing. Now!

Isabel, shocked by the ferocity of her mother's voice, her wide eyes, let the bone fall from her grip and exploded into tears.

What had she done wrong? She'd found the mask, after all; it was hers. So what if Olivia wanted it; if only her father was there!

Laura grabbed Isabel tightly in her arms, and Isabel burst afresh into tears.

I told her to leave it on the beach, Olivia remarked.

Laura smothered Isabel in her dress. She hadn't meant to scream; she wished she had remained calm.

Honey, you did nothing wrong, she soothed.

Olivia scratched the back of her right leg with the toe of her left; her braid was in her mouth again.

Thank you, her mother mouthed the words over Isabel's

head. Olivia kicked at the grass and wandered toward the back of the house. Isabel was wailing now; it was time for her nap besides.

That night, Isabel would tell her father on the phone how Mommy used a word she wasn't allow to (*fuck, fuck, fuck*), and her father in his office in Montreal said that was okay, even Mommy sometimes slips.

The squad car arrived an hour later. Laura had gotten Isabel down for a nap. A cup of chamomile tea for her own nerves. The lights flashed silently in the drive. A large man with red curls and muttonchops came to the screen door. Isabel had woken, excited now, and wanted to tell everyone *she* (not Olivia) was the one who found the thing.

Yes, dear, her mother said. Olivia kicked her sister and muttered for her to shut up.

But I found the merman's mask!

Enough, Laura said and opened the screen door.

Bunty Phillips stepped inside and removed his hat. He wore a blue windbreaker. The room seemed suddenly cramped by his presence. Laura told him where the pelvis was and pointed through the window toward the front lawn.

May I talk to the girls? he asked. Procedure, he explained.

Olivia stepped forward from behind her mother. Laura held her shoulders from behind.

You were with your sister?

Yes sir.

But she was the one who found it?

Olivia nodded.

How far down the beach?

By the estuary.

Isabel squirmed in front of her mother too.

Bunty squatted down to Isabel's level and ran a hand through his reddish curls. He twirled his hat in one hand, like a Frisbee. He had pale blue eyes, a double chin. His hair looked like copper wires.

You two want to show us exactly where you found it?

Do they have to? Laura protested. Really?

Bunty glanced toward the living room window and the water beyond. The bluefish were running that time of year. That was all he could think about, how, on a fine day like this, he'd be out on the water dropping his lines. But his boat had been in dry dock since last October, and his job had become that of a messenger boy, a pickup man, driving up and down the whole goddamn coast, collecting things in plastic bags and charting them with the GPS the government had loaned him. Frankly, he was sick of it.

Bunty lifted himself off his knees and set his hat back on his head.

No, he exhaled. They don't have to.

Olivia glanced from Bunty to her mother. Bunty watched her, the older daughter. His own grandchild was about her age.

He didn't ask anything else. He left his number, a couple of pamphlets, went out to the yard, put on his protective gloves, sealed the bone in plastic, and wrote the address and the time it was found (he'd check the coordinates later). Before he left, he knocked on the door again and asked for Isabel.

Her mother brought her to the screen door, and Bunty squatted once more to her level.

You know something, he said through the screen. You were right after all. That *is* the merman's mask.

A toothy smile erupted on Isabel's face, and she turned it up to her mother.

See. I told you.

Yes, honey. Her mother smiled and looked at Bunty through the screen and thanked him with her eyes.

He climbed back into the squad car. They all watched him go. What a day it had been already—and it was not yet noon.

The socket in the pelvis where the femur joins the ilium is called the "acetabulum." In Latin it means "vinegar cup." The indentation is deep and cup-shaped and directed downward and outward and forward. It was this part of the ilium that was flown to a lab in Indiana, and there all the joined bones were pulverized and tested for weeks. And it wasn't until almost July when Ana Gathreaux received the phone call from the head pathologist in Halifax. She was in her lab at the time. The man's voice was measured. Was she alone? he asked. (Yes.) Was she sitting down? (No.)

You might, he said, want to have a seat.

They'd identified Russell's remains. The rest she didn't hear. Was it relief she felt, or an oceanic sadness, like a wave collapsing on the sand, with nowhere now to crawl to but back under the sea? The pathologist talked for a while longer, but his words no longer cohered; they seemed to Ana like tiny black beads falling out of the receiver and spilling over the floor— pearls on a necklace, bouncing out the door. She said she'd have to call him back, she had to hang up now. Before she did, she asked one thing: Are you positive it's him?

She both wanted, and didn't want, to hear his answer.

The man said: One hundred percent.

I've got to go now, she whispered.

The man said he understood and started to leave a number for her to call back, but she hung up before the last digit.

When Ana mist-netted birds in the field, the most exciting part—she couldn't deny it—was seeing what had flown into her nets. Every fifteen minutes, whether she was in Montauk or upstate New York or on Dauphin Island, she checked the black nylon nets to see what the wind had brought. Each time felt as if she'd been dealt a fresh hand of cards: a Cedar Waxwing here, a Veery there, a Black-throated Blue Warbler. Each bird she'd extract with the same meticulous care, determining which way it had gotten caught in the first place. She'd take the bird by the legs, free the toes first, disentangle the wings or the tail, and sometimes she'd have to work the netting free from the forks of the bird's tongue—a nasty job, best accomplished with a safety pin. Once she'd untangled the bird, she held it in her hands, its legs pressed between her fingers, wings free. They always tried to fly immediately but when they realized they couldn't, they settled down and sat on her middle finger, their hearts beating wildly, their beaks open from stress. Ana often wondered what the birds thought of her—this enormous, willful predator, who manipulated their wings, plucked a feather or two, pricked them for blood, and then—just as suddenly—let them free. Once in a great while she mist-netted birds who'd been banded before (the tiny aluminum bracelets already on their legs). The birds who'd been caught and released before seemed—perhaps it was her imagination—a bit calmer, as if they were old hands at it and knew no harm would befall them.

When a bird, even something as large as a towhee or a jay, sat on her fingers, the weight seemed negligible. This had always surprised Ana more than anything: it still did. A warbler was lighter than half an ounce, lighter than a letter in an envelope with a postage stamp. At the banding stations, her assistants helped with the calipers, the bands, the scales, the pipettes for collecting blood. After they'd done all the recording, she'd open her palm and let the bird escape.

This was the moment that gave Ana—still—the most pleasure. The banded bird, palpitating, exhausted, was given its life back again. And there was always that moment when the bird sat warily, unable to understand its sudden freedom, not sure if it was being tricked again. If Ana looked away for but a split second, the bird would fly. Yet if she gazed right at it, the bird usually stayed put. It was often impossible actually to *see* the moment of flight. She could never look dead straight at the thing but only through indirection, through *not looking,* through almost forgetting, could she experience the bird's flight.

Back in the lab, she collected all her sparrows—even Rothschild, who'd recovered over the winter and was healthy again. She brought them in one cage down to the lobby, where Armand went outside to hail a cab. The streets were already wilting in New York City, the sky a wash of brown. The Mister Softee truck on Washington Square kept playing its idiot theme.

Armand held the cab door open and helped her inside with the cage.

You are going with all of them?

Yes, she said.

He leaned down to the cage and waved to the birds *au revoir,* then closed the door and stepped back to the curb.

The driver wore an olive turban. The sun fell through trees along the Belt Parkway. Some people were flying box kites beside the Verrazano Narrows Bridge. She directed the driver all the way out to Jamaica Bay, along the Cross Bay Boulevard, and into the wildlife refuge. The afternoon was growing old. Ana paid the driver and climbed from the cab. He asked if he should wait, and she told him no, don't bother.

She hoofed her cage to the farthest point of the refuge. Some late birders looked suspiciously at her caged sparrows. The breeze was stiff off the channel. When she'd walked as far as she could, she set the cage in the sand and opened the wire door. The birds didn't fly right away. They hopped around and seemed to sniff the breeze. That was the strange thing. Even Rothschild stayed put.

She walked away and sat at a distance on a park bench, shivering, and didn't watch on purpose. The sun was a pale red ball dropping through smog, the towers of the city already lit up in the west. Planes kept looming out of Kennedy. In another twenty minutes, all her birds had flown.

TWENTY·ONE

In summer on Trachis Island, the beach plums blossomed, the blue flag, the marsh forget-me-nots. Ferries churned in the harbor. The summer crowds returned in increments. All over the island, houses were opened, aired, storm windows replaced with screens. Everywhere lay reminders of the crash: the military trucks, the Jeeps, the new construction of Quonset huts at the naval yard. The ferries brought tour buses from the mainland, more than ever before, filled not with the usual island hoppers but with people who'd come specifically to see the site of the crash. Who would have predicted such a grim attraction at Caginish Point? During the high season the ferries grew so overbooked they had to add two extra sailings each day.

At Caginish, tourists stumbled off buses, blinked in the sun, digital cameras and video recorders strapped around necks. The men always led the way, marching toward the rocks as if *this* was their domain (mechanical failure, aviation disaster) while the women lagged behind with children and pocket-books. The Japanese tourists were the quietest, the quickest, the most respectful. The Americans the loudest. The Dutch always stayed at the spot the longest, sometimes with bagged lunches brought from the mainland. The drivers stood outside their buses, smoking, talking. The passenger cars arrived in such numbers that the Trachis Town Board debated whether to enlarge the parking lot and pave the paths that wound down to the sea. Some suggested they start to charge a fee.

The anniversary of the crash arrived. There were ceremonies on the island. Candlelight vigils, the ringing of ship bells for each passenger that had perished. And on the mainland in Halifax, dignitaries gave speeches, families gathered, the Symphony Nova Scotia played a piece of music that had been found floating on the waters: Richard Strauss's *Metamorphoses: A Study for Twenty-three Solo Strings.*

That first year, Kevin Gearns closed the inn the week of the crash. He was surprised—and pleased—that some of the guests returned, those who'd been there the year before. Diana Olmstead drove up one afternoon with two friends and gave Kevin a bear hug. The Italian couple dropped in to say hello. The black family from Brooklyn spent a night at the inn, at Kevin's insistence: they wanted to see the sun rise out of the ocean the next morning.

That autumn passed. The next winter. The parking lot at Caginish was paved and expanded with funds from Ottawa. A marble memorial was ceremonially set in place, engraved with the name of each passenger on the flight. The second-year anniversary arrived, and some of the same people returned to

Trachis Inn. By the third year, it had become something of a tradition. Diana Olmstead sent out invitations and e-mails; and Kevin opened the inn only for those who'd been on the island that first week. Douglas, who'd returned by now, was skeptical at first. Who would want to come back to the site of such anguish, such memories? Yet Kevin understood the powers of the water, the beauty of the island, and why, despite everything, a few of them would want to return.

It was now the fifth-year anniversary, and they were coming once more. Five years, and so much had changed! Yet this one week in late September always seemed the same—the weather clear and flawless, the ocean a dark ultramarine. That morning Kevin picked white phlox and zinnias and distributed them in each of the cottages. In the early afternoon, he printed menus for that evening's meal. He'd asked Douglas *four* times to do it—he was so much better with the fonts and the printer—but Douglas, of course, had forgotten.

Kevin walked into the dining room with the menu. Claartija deJong stood stretching by the double glass doors, one leg on the floor, the other balanced on a chair. She wore a white chef's outfit, her hair pulled back with a blue rubber band.

Here it is, Kevin announced, flapping the menu as if to dry.

The fonts were too small, but they'd have to do. He handed the piece of paper to Claartija, who inspected the list:

Hen of the Wood Mushroom Duxelles on Toast Points
Corn Chowder
Goose Confit
Coulibiac of Nova Scotia Salmon / Venison Roast

Grilled Haricots Verts
Fresh Field Green Vinaigrette with Trachis Island Chèvre
Seasonal Fruit / Mont Blanc Vanilla Cream

He and Claartija had prepared the meal for days, the couli-biac in parchment paper, the venison marinated in buttermilk; and here was the final menu. Everything was ready now in the kitchen. Everything either prepped or cooked or simmering on the stove.

Claartija handed him back the piece of paper. It looks all right, she said.

Kevin waited for more. What he wanted her to notice—but she hadn't yet—was that all the elements were represented in the menu: something from the air (the goose), the land (the venison), the sea (the salmon), the soil itself (potatoes, fungus, greens). But Claartija said nothing, and he doubted anyone else would notice. Years ago it might have mattered—back when he'd first opened the inn and hovered outside the dining room door hoping to hear comments about his cooking. It stung him then to see a plate returned with food still on it. Yet not anymore. He cooked because he loved to, because it gave *him* pleasure. If someone noticed the subtleties of his cuisine, all the better. The important thing was: They enjoy the food.

Kevin took the menu, and Claartija dropped her foot from the chair.

I just riced the chestnuts for the Mont Blanc, she said.

Did you follow the recipe?

She rolled her eyes.

Sorry, Kevin said.

The roast went in about fifteen minutes ago.

Kevin was about to say something else when the deafening

roar of the lawn mower drowned out his voice. Douglas passed the window just then on the riding mower. They watched him through the screens in his muscle shirt, backing up, going forward, checking the swath he'd just cut. He wore bright orange ear protectors; he didn't even notice them standing inside the dining room four feet away.

Kevin shook his head after he'd gone. He'll do that all afternoon if he has his way.

What's with him and that machine? Claartija asked.

Kevin shrugged. It's his form of relaxation. Some people do yoga. He does mow-ga.

Claartija made a face. Awf, she said and flicked a finger at his arm. I've got things to do.

Kevin smirked; Claartija headed back to the kitchen.

Don't forget to put water in the bottom of the roasting pan, he added.

Ah Verdomme! she said and threw a hand in the air.

Kevin watched her go; he recognized the borrowed gesture and was secretly pleased. He turned toward the stairs. He needed to shave and shower before the guests arrived.

The first few years, the anniversaries were solemn. The second year hardly anyone showed up. Yet something happened around the third year. People stopped coming out of obligation or a sense of deep bereavement. They told stories around the table. They laughed. They spoke—for the first time—of the future. The weekend was no longer so reverential or sober. Claartija, who'd been living at the inn for almost two years now, took them out in the Sunfish on the water. They lay on the beach for an afternoon or barbecued in the evening. Kevin imagined they came partly to remember. But also, partly, to relax.

That fifth year, Ana Gathreaux made the journey from Manhattan. The drive took at least two days. If she'd caught the ferry in Bar Harbor it would have been shorter, but Ana liked traveling overland, through the Maine forests, past Katahdin— the haunt of Russell's Bicknell's Thrush—up to Houlton, where she crossed the border into New Brunswick. She'd done the drive twice now. Once at the first-year anniversary with her mother-in-law, and again the third year. She enjoyed driving alone, at the end of summer, feeling the continent slip beneath the wheels of her rented car, smelling the ripe fields through the window, the goldenrod, corn, and hay—and watching the migrants along the way heading in the opposite direction. Crossing into Canada, she always felt as if she'd left a piece of herself behind there at the border and once through customs, she felt a little lighter, shorn of a slight percentage of body weight? Memory? Her work? She didn't know which. But during those first empty miles on Highway 2, sunlight splashing the pavement, she couldn't help but smile, as if she'd somehow gotten away—from what, she couldn't say.

This year, however, she hadn't come alone. She'd driven from New York City with Pars Mansoor. They spent a night in a roadside motel in the Maine woods. In Moncton, they visited Magnetic Hill and drove up and down it six whole times. They stopped in Great Village, Pars wanting to see Elizabeth Bishop's childhood home. In Truro, they watched the tidal bore, the long tides rushing in from the sea. It was something of a vacation for them both. They spent the last night outside New Glasgow before heading down to the South Shore.

Each time Ana arrived on Trachis Island she went first to Caginish Point. She'd bring flowers to the spot, bouquets she'd collected along the way. That year was no different, and she and Pars drove to the end of the island first. Ana brought a bouquet of wild lupines and blue aster. Pars brought a wreath of lavender for his niece. Earlier that summer, a colleague at the Smithsonian had named a previously undescribed bee-eater after Russell—the trinomial part of the name at least. Years before he'd brought the specimen back from one of his collecting trips in Southeast Asia. The naming was really quite an honor, and Ana had framed the article from *The Auk* alongside a photograph of the bird and brought it to Trachis. It was a bit sentimental, she realized, but who cared? She leaned the framed article against the marble monument, alongside all the other flowers and stones and melted candles. She placed her own bouquet against the glass. Pars laid his lavender wreath beside it.

By the time they arrived at Trachis Inn, it was already four in the afternoon. The keys to their cottages were left in the office. Ana was ravenous. They hadn't eaten since an Irving station outside Antigonish. She'd been saving herself for one of Kevin Gearns's meals.

TWENTY-TWO

And now the sun lowered over Trachis and poured into the dining room. The late afternoon light—chill and Septemberish—glimmered against each spoon and glass and wine bottle. Diana Olmstead shaded her eyes against the glare. Pars Mansoor did as well. Ana Gathreaux sat across from him. A tall boy with an earring and unruly red hair sat beside Claartija. The meal had already begun, the mushroom appetizer, the corn chowder, the bread, the wine. Kevin stood outside the kitchen door, uncorking another bottle of Cloudy Bay. They were calling for him to join them.

Just a minute, he shouted.

He draped a towel over his wrist and walked around the table refilling glasses.

Diana Olmstead grabbed his arm. You *must* sit down now.

One more thing, he said. He had to check on the roast, the vinaigrette.

Douglas rose from his chair and went around the table and put both hands on Kevin's shoulders. He steered him across the room to a seat at the head of the table, then lowered him into the chair.

Kevin blushed slightly. He didn't like being there—at the head of the table—but it was the only seat left. Douglas returned to his place and shook his head across the table. The sun was on the lip of the ocean now. Everyone's face looked flushed in the orange glow.

Diana Olmstead began a toast. Every year she did the same, and usually they had a moment of silence before the meal, and sometimes after. She had her glass lifted and was talking now about her granddaughter, how she was raising monarch butterflies for a school project. Ana listened. How it was related to all of them—the pupae, the cocoon, the chrysalis—she wasn't sure. But it was five years now, Diana Olmstead reminded them, and like the caterpillar, all things change. Had it been that long? Ana marveled, holding the stem of her wineglass, for sometimes it felt as if Russell had left her the day before, or a week before, that he'd just stepped out the door for a quart of milk and would be back soon. But other times it seemed that decades had passed, that he was another life she once lived, long ago. Back then, five years ago, she thought she'd never eat again, never have a moment of happiness, never be able *not* to think about him. Yet here she was now, sitting at a table with the others, holding her glass in the air.

She leaned back and gazed at Claartija at the opposite end of the table. How radiant the girl looked, Ana thought, in her green dress and silver earrings. How different from the first time on the island. Her hair had grown long and brown; her arms tanned, and the brow ring was gone. She was mouthing something to the boy beside her, and Ana felt a certain wistfulness. For what exactly: Youth? The boyfriend? For Claartija herself? Ana remembered herself at that age, the boyfriends, her father. Claartija had grown so much in five years, and look what she'd turned into!

Diana Olmstead finished her toast. The sun dropped behind the bluff, and the room fell into shadow. They all clinked glasses and drank. Kevin stood and passed around small plates of goose confit. Pars took his dish and lifted his head to Kevin.

What if I want my goose *without* feet? he asked.

Kevin looked confused a moment; then Pars held a napkin to his mouth.

Ana groaned. Kevin shook his head.

But the feet *are* the best part, Kevin replied.

Pars watched Ana across the table. She smiled wryly at him; it made him feel the smallest bit warm inside. How it thrilled him to see her smile, for *him* to make her smile. For two years, each time he saw her in Manhattan or Berkeley, she had looked perpetually distracted, as if she were always working out some impossible algebra equation in her head. Only recently did she seem more present, more relaxed, as if something unmeasurable had lifted from her soul. At Magnetic Hill the day before in Moncton, she'd rolled down the window and hung herself out in the breeze, and screamed as the car was going backward; and for a moment Pars thought: This is what Ana looked like when she was eight years old, before the first worry: how one never quite loses the face of one's childhood, how it sneaks into the creases and folds at times unannounced, unbidden, as it had that afternoon. And now, looking across the table at her, her hand over her mouth, her eyes shining, Pars saw it again: Ana at sixteen, at five. Ana at fifty. Ana when her husband married her. Pars felt incredibly close to him; he was always the third party in the room, this man named Russell. His name the word for what a bird does in the dark. He was there too, in that face; all of it in Ana, in a flash.

Kevin brought out more Sauvignon Blanc, and an Oregon Pinot Noir. He handed a bottle of Australian Shiraz to Pars.

In your honor, Kevin said.

Pars studied the label. His grandfather had made his own wine from the sweet amber grapes named after the city. But the Shiraz now, he explained, had little in common, unfortunately, with the original Persian grape.

Just then the kitchen door swung open and the odor of the roast filled the room. Sheila Quinn brought the silver tray to the table and set it down in the center among the other dishes. Ana closed her eyes and thought of her parents' house on Long Island and the pot roast her mother used to make on Sundays when her grandparents visited from Queens. Claartija was transported briefly back to holiday meals at her home in southern Holland; for once, there was no fighting, and a *Gestoofde runderlappen* steamed on the table. Pars too was reminded of the tiny kitchen and the *Abgousht* his mother used to make, the heady odor of onions and sumac and lamb stewed for hours.

Outside, twilight lingered in the trees. Crickets shirred on the lawn. Claartija stood and went around the table lighting candles. They all noticed her. Not just Ana but Pars too and Diana Olmstead and Douglas, and they looked at each other across the table and seemed to share the same thought: that she belonged to all of them somehow. Douglas stood and helped her with the candles. Kevin brought in the coulibiac on a tray. Claartija made room for it on the table, the puff pastry steaming and golden in the candlelight.

They ate. They talked. The candles flickered and swayed. Everyone tasted the roast—except Diana Olmstead, of course, who was a vegetarian. The meat was perfectly prepared. Kevin had no appetite himself; rarely did he after a day in the kitchen. But people were sopping up juices from their plates with bits of bread. Douglas was lost in conversation with Ana. Pars was telling Diana Olmstead the word for popcorn in Persian was "elephant farts." Kevin looked up and caught Claartija's eye across the table, and she winked at him, then turned and whispered something into her boyfriend's ear. He seemed to Kevin a decent boy—quiet, attentive, his red hair always falling into his eyes. He played bass guitar in clubs off the island, and Claartija traveled sometimes as far as Halifax to watch his indie rock band. She was five years older than he, and he followed her around the inn like a puppy. Who could have predicted that Bunty Phillips's youngest son would wear a silver stud in one ear and spend summer nights with a Dutch girl who lived with Kevin and Douglas at Trachis Inn? It would have seemed unthinkable only a few years ago. When Kevin ran into Bunty in town now, they exchanged pleasantries but avoided the topic—though both of them knew exactly what was going on.

* * *

Later, after the salad, and the cheese and the roasted nuts, after the ice wine from Pictou, and the Mont Blanc, the candles guttered in their globes. The tablecloth lay strewn with bits of bread and wine corks and almond shells. Sheila cleared the dishes, and Claartija rose to help, but Douglas made her sit. Outside, night had fallen; and in the dining room, they could hear the surf through the closed doors. Claartija and her boyfriend wandered out to the terrace. Diana Olmstead rose and stretched. A minute later, Claartija came running into the room.

You've got to see the moon! she exclaimed, then turned back outside.

Ana looked at Pars. They both rose with their wineglasses. Everyone else drifted out to the lawn. The night was clear and a full moon was just lifting out of the ocean, orange and luminous, dripping a liquid gold leaf into the sea.

It's a harvest moon, Ana commented to no one in particular.

Why is it so large? Claartija asked.

The atmosphere does that, Ana explained. All the gases act as a magnifying glass. Once it gets higher, it won't look as big.

Douglas came out with two lawn chairs and blankets, and Diana Olmstead thanked him and lowered herself into a chair. Claartija sat cross-legged in the grass; her boyfriend huddled near her, brushing hair from his face. Ana slipped her hand into Pars's.

On a clear autumn night like this, with the moon full, Ana and her husband used to sit on the roof of their loft looking at the disk of the moon through spotting scopes mounted on tripods. You could tell the rough density of migrating birds by how many you counted in an hour flying across the face of the moon. Once Ana had participated in a moon-watching survey over the Gulf of Mexico. Two hundred volunteers, staring through opticals at the moon.

Ana told the others about the study, about how you could actually see birds migrating in the dark.

Come on, Claartija said.

It's really fairly simple, Ana explained. All you need is a twenty-powered scope, or even a pair of field glasses sometimes works.

Claartija's boyfriend swept hair from his eyes. Could we try it? he asked.

Ana shrugged. It takes a bit of training.

Pars tamped out his cigarette. What better night than this? he asked.

Well. Ana turned to Kevin. Do you have any binoculars?

Kevin seemed startled by the question. He'd been sitting in the grass, leaning on his elbows, staring up at the moon.

Sorry? he said and blushed in the dark.

Binoculars, Ana repeated.

Yes, Douglas answered. He has at least two pairs.

Douglas put his hands on his knees and stood. I'll get them, he said.

Do you know where they are? Kevin asked.

Yes, Douglas said, walking away.

One's in the library, Kevin shouted.

I *know.*

And bring the telescope.

Kevin turned to Ana. Will that work?

I guess we'll see, Ana said. She stood as well. Her Swarovskis were in the cottage. She brought them with her whenever she traveled now; she'd even brought a pair of Nikons for Pars to use on the trip. She was teaching him the names of North American birds.

A few minutes later, Douglas returned with the binoculars and the telescope. Ana came back too. They distributed the opticals; only Diana Olmstead declined. The moon had lifted clear off the water now and hung full-blown above the horizon. Ana told them to turn the focus ring all the way open and keep as still as possible. The slightest movement would make the image tremble.

Claartija brought the binoculars to her face.

I can't see anything, she complained.

You've got to be very still and very patient, Ana said. Ideally we should be using tripods. The best way is to lie down and put the glasses to your face and then control your breath.

Ana lay down on her back. The lawn was still warm from the day. Pars lay next to her; she could hear his breath nearby. Claartija sat on the opposite side, and Claartija's boyfriend beside her. Kevin stood fooling with the knobs of his telescope, trying to get a smaller image of the moon. After all that time of his wanting the telescope, Douglas had finally gotten him one a few years earlier. Yet Kevin never really took to the instrument and never found anything more than Mars and Venus. He preferred his focus on the earth, at his feet, on his plants. He left the constellations to Douglas.

Oscar wandered over and stood panting above them. He leaned down and licked Claartija's boyfriend on the face.

Jesus! he screamed.

What?

The dog, he surprised me.

He's just saying hello, Claartija said. Go away, Oscar.

She reached up and rubbed his chest, then pushed him gently aside.

Pars kept very still. Through his binoculars, the moon was amazingly bright, a white sheet that shivered each time he inhaled.

I see a big crater, he announced.

Does it have rays emanating from it? Ana asked.

Yes, he said, it does.

That's Tycho, Ana said. When you do this officially, she explained, you use Tycho as a reference for the size of the bird and the direction it's flying.

We're not official, are we? Pars asked.

God, I should hope not, Kevin muttered.

They grew quiet. They all watched. They all waited, eyes to lenses. The crickets had started again in the grass. The wind blew from the north. Ana knew: the smallest songbird could be detected at a distance of two kilometers, flying across the face of the moon. Through the binoculars, the bird appears the size of a period at the end of a sentence: a small fleck, hardly noticeable, a shutter opening and closing too fast even to register. But if you took the time and were still enough, and your eyes were completely open, you'd see it. As Ana did just then. Her first bird of the night.

I got one, she said, her voice muted behind the binoculars.

This is impossible, Claartija moaned.

Keep looking, Douglas encouraged.

Pars, who'd been holding his breath for almost a full minute now, saw something flash across the moon.

I think I saw one.

Good, Ana said.

I'm not sure, though, he added.

The last time Ana had moon-watched was with Russell on Dauphin Island in the Gulf of Mexico. Russell kept calling out the names of birds that passed. Not that he could identify them by their shape (they moved too quickly) but because he was great at vocalization—not his own but the birds': He knew all their flight calls. *Indigo Bunting!* he'd shout. *Boat-tailed Grackle, Snowy Egret.* Ana was impressed—and a bit annoyed—at his ability to hear their calls in the dark. It was as if he were picking sounds out of the night that no one else knew existed.

Claartjia's boyfriend shouted: There! I think I saw one! Just a dot!

He put down his glasses and rubbed his eyes.

Ana kept seeing them now, a steady stream of migrants, but said nothing. She could even make out a few of their forms. A woodcock, a few passerines. The night was full of migrants. If you saw thirty birds in one hour cross the moon, it was a heavily trafficked night—because you were seeing only a tiny fraction of the night sky (one one-hundredth of the horizon). Already Ana had seen about ten birds in as many minutes, and she knew, out in the darkness, beyond the moon's face, the night was restless with birds. Millions of them, scattering all over the sky.

Pars saw another one. Then Claartija's boyfriend. Finally Kevin saw something in the lens of the telescope. So small. So insignificant. He wasn't sure what it was.

The dog sat beside Claartija. Then Claartija gave up, set the binoculars on her stomach, and lay on her back in the grass, her hand grazing her boyfriend's arm. Pars kept watching; he was up to six birds now. Diana Olmstead sat nearby in her chair and observed them all lying on the lawn, staring at the sky. She fingered her prayer beads in the dark and gazed up at the moon as well. She needed no binoculars. She felt no need actually to *see* the birds. She knew they were there. Just because you couldn't see something didn't mean it *wasn't* there. She fingered each bead between her thumb and forefinger. The night smelled of jasmine, of musk roses. She looked up at the platinum moon and knew they were out there—all of them—between the sea and the earth and the sky.

TWENTY·THREE

How is a story like a bird? It keeps us aloft. It flies. It goes from one place and lands at another, seemingly at random. But its movements are carefully choreographed, and if you look closely, you'll know exactly where it will next perch.

Later that night, after the guests returned to their rooms, after the kitchen was cleaned, the pots scrubbed, the dishes stacked and stored, Kevin made a final sweep of the house, shutting lamps and closing doors. He climbed upstairs to the master bedroom. Douglas was already under the covers with the lights off. With the excitement of the dinner, and the house partly full again, Kevin knew he wouldn't easily get to sleep—not right away at least. He tiptoed to the window and sat in the seat and surveyed the lawn. Trees soughed outside, the sea sparkled in the night. Kevin heard Douglas ask from the bed: Is everything all right?

Fine, Kevin answered.

All of them have gone to bed?

Uh-hmm.

Kevin looked up at the moon. It had drifted now into a web of diaphanous clouds.

After a moment Douglas asked: What is it?

Nothing, Kevin replied.

Douglas waited. He knew, nights like this, all Kevin needed was the slightest prompting. And after a moment, sure enough, Kevin said: I was just thinking, that's all.

Douglas silently shook his head; sometimes Kevin was so predictable.

And what were you thinking? he asked.

About the kingfishers.

Douglas sighed and threw off the covers and crossed the room. What had always delighted and infuriated him about Kevin were his grand classical references that seemed to come out of the blue. He sat beside him now in the window seat and crossed his ankles; and they both looked over the lawn a moment without speaking.

Well, Douglas finally said, leaning against the wall, are you going to tell me about the kingfishers? This must be a Greek story, right?

Yes. Kevin nodded, pleased. It's the myth of the halcyon days.

And then he began to tell Douglas the story—as Douglas knew he would. It was all about a queen named Alcyone and a king named Ceyx, who lived on an island in the Aegean, and how they bragged about their perfect love, and how the gods, angered by their boasting, shipwrecked the king at sea. Kevin told Douglas about the shipwreck and how afterward, when the king's body floated back to shore, Queen Alcyone, in her awful grief, leapt into the sea. Yet before she hit the water, the gods took pity on the queen and turned her into a bird: a kingfisher. She sprouted wings, a tail, a large beak, and then she kissed the king's dead lips with her beak, and he came alive and changed right then into a kingfisher too. They flew off together, the king and queen, and each year for a week in winter, Kevin explained, the gods calmed the oceans so the two birds could nest on the open sea. Those days of calm, Kevin said, were called "halcyon days," because the word in Greek for kingfisher was "halcyon"; and that's where the phrase comes from—the halcyon days—from the kingfishers.

And? Douglas asked from the dark. He was waiting now for more.

That's all. Kevin shrugged.

He could have told Douglas about Ovid's version of the myth, or how kingfishers didn't really nest on the water, and certainly not in winter, but instead he stopped there. The ocean was churning in the dark, the night colder now. The dinner had been a success, and for that Kevin was thankful. He rose and stretched, then locked the window against the chill and started across the room, but stopped and came back to the window seat.

Are you coming? he asked.

He held a hand out in the dark; and Douglas, silhouetted momentarily against the sea, nodded and reached for his hand and said, yes, he was coming at last to bed.

I n April, he perched on a witch hazel branch, shivering, one eye
closed, waiting for the sun to warm his wings. The night had
been particularly cold, the winter long, the fishing scarce.
He'd been alone all the time.

When the sun appeared, the warmth felt good on his wings. He
lifted from his perch, wheeled, then cackled over the river, studying the
surface for the slightest flash: a trout, a small shad, a frog. He lit on
a willow snag downriver and sunned himself, raised his tail, shat,
and called again. The days were growing longer now, the alewives
ascending the streams. The year before, he'd built his nest near the
estuary in a seam of clay, and soon—if she returned—the time would
come for a new nest along the bank.

The kingfisher fished all morning. He returned to the willow snag
at noon; slept, then woke shortly after, startled by the call. Was it
she? They hadn't seen each other since the summer before.

He dropped from the branch, called, winged downriver, his image *doubled in the water. He heard the call again, closer now. If she returned, he'd dive into the river, greet her with a fish, fly around her, feed her beak to beak. If she returned, he'd begin to excavate a new nest, claw clay out of the earth, arrange the perfect pile of fish bones to lay their eggs upon.*

He pumped his wings harder now. He heard the cackle closer, louder, more insistent. He recognized her voice. She was hurling her way upriver.

Any moment now: she'd fly into his vision.

In Gratitude

Many people contributed to the creation of this fiction. To the following I owe a tremendous debt: Paul Sweet at the American Museum of Natural History; Ursula Munro at the University of Technology in Sydney; Chris Rimmer and Kent McFarland at Vermont Institute of Natural Science; John Phillips at Virginia Polytechnic Institute; Allison Sloan and New York City Audubon's Project Safe Flight. Barry MacKay and Dale Dyer, Stephen Kimber for his work *Flight 111*, Dr. Kathy Dardeck, Jonathan Springer, Carol Mann for *all* her higher guidance. Thanks to Mohktar Paki, Jen Chen, Adam Levy, and Michael Finckel. The MacDowell Colony, the Corporation of Yaddo, and the Vermont Arts Council. Special gratitude to Nancy Zafris, Stephen Hubbell, Tim Miller, Lisa Dickey, Catherine Bush, Anna deVries, Alexis Gargagliano, and Betsy Lerner. And, as always, the ever-sage Nan Graham.

Finally, my deepest debt is to Dona Ann McAdams, copilot, partner in flight.

ABOUT THE AUTHOR

BRAD KESSLER is the author of *Lick Creek* and *The Woodcutter's Christmas*, as well as several award-winning children's books. He is the recipient of a National Endowment for the Arts grant, and his work has appeared in numerous major periodicals, such as *The New Yorker*, *The New York Times Magazine*, and *The Nation*.